Desert Gothic

The

Iowa

Short

Fiction

Award

In honor of James O. Freedman

University

of Iowa Press

Iowa City

Don
Waters

Desert
Gothic

University of Iowa Press, Iowa City 52242
Copyright © 2007 by Don Waters
www.uiowapress.org

Printed in the United States of America

The University of Iowa Press is a member of Green Press
Initiative and is committed to preserving natural resources.

Printed on acid-free paper

Library of Congress Cataloging-in-Publication Data
Waters, Don, 1974–
    Desert gothic / by Don Waters.
        p.   cm.—(The Iowa short fiction award)
    ISBN-13: 978-1-58729-624-6 (pbk.)
    ISBN-10: 1-58729-624-1 (pbk.)
    I. Title.
    PS3623.A8688D47   2007   2007008812
    813'.6—dc22

For my mother, Donna Lee

Contents

ACKNOWLEDGEMENTS

I owe thanks to the following people for their support, encouragement, and guidance: Heather Schroder, Robert Glück, Dennis Cooper, Blake Nelson, Peter Dubé, Erin Johansson, Ralph Morgan, and especially Ben Fountain. Huge thanks to KJ Page for her bigheartedness. My dear pal Josh Benke provided much insight and humor. Emily Benke was extraordinarily helpful with information about marathon running. I want to acknowledge Luis Alberto Urrea and Charles Bowden for their tremendous and rousing border writing; I'd also like to pay tribute to the late, great Edward Abbey, who left his heart in the desert. A Jentel Residency Fellowship afforded me the time to clean up several of these stories. Thanks to my family, as always. And enormous thanks, for her patience and love, to my partner, my collaborator, Robin Romm.

"What to Do with the Dead" and "Mr. Epstein and the Dealer" appeared in the *Southwest Review*. "Sheets" and "Little Sins" appeared in *Grain*. "Blood Management" appeared in the *Santa Monica Review*. "Holiday at the Shamrock" appeared in the *Cimarron Review*. "The Bulls at San Luis" appeared in *StoryQuarterly*. "Mormons in Heat" appeared in the *Kenyon Review*. "Mineral and Steel" appeared in *Epoch*. "Dan Buck" appeared in the *Greensboro Review*.

Desert Gothic

What
to Do
with the
Dead

Melvin, my coworker, sometimes talked ghosts while preparing a burn.

"So look, friends say it's strange, but there's a clause in my will for Springer," he told me. "And I wanted your opinion about it," he went on, "whether or not, you know, it's strange?"

Springer was a large part of Melvin's life, a calico I'd heard much about. I didn't have an opinion one way or the other. To me, whatever Melvin wanted: fine. Though I'd only known him a short time, it was clear Melvin, a squat, fortyish, high-foreheaded man, was a champion of animal companionship. I'd also heard talk from the grounds crew that Melvin was a refugee fresh from a war-torn marriage, which helped explain his devotion.

"It's decided that when Springer goes there's a spot for him in my entertainment center," he said, adding, as if to impress me, "behind glass."

Melvin tapped the retort's gauge, inspecting the temperature. A glowing ball of orange light filled the retort's small rectangular window as it climbed toward sixteen hundred degrees.

"And when I go, I've requested that Springer be mixed in with me. For interment I've decided—"

Melvin lifted his hand, his ginger-colored eyes widening. He carefully scanned the plain industrial room.

"Did you feel that?" he asked. "The breeze?"

He was talking ghosts again and I didn't like it. I didn't believe in ghosts, or spirits, or gods. I painted. Life was filled with too many choices.

Melvin massaged his forearms, saying, "Now that was something."

I was across the room on a hard metal stool, trying to copy down the delivery addresses of yesterday's burns. A black binder hung via wire from the wall. Lists of names corresponded to dates of death. Attached was a pencil, a chipped nub, which gave my hand cramps.

The pencil's tip hovered over a street that didn't match my directory. I didn't recognize the name. In fact, where the hell was Choking, Nevada? I looked at the form again. Mary Ellis, age thirty. Requested delivery address: Choking. A joke? I was more annoyed that I didn't know where Choking was than by the fact that Mary Ellis was a thirty-year-old overdose.

All together, there were four deliveries, including the capsule now resting on the retort's mechanical lift.

"Who's going in?" Melvin asked.

I picked fuzz from my lip. "A man named Edward Yoo."

"Makes sense, another Chinese bribe," Melvin said. "The man's restless. I hope his family gave him a spendy send-off. That was probably him, just now, Edward Yoo."

I wanted to ask Melvin how he figured that but didn't.

Every few weeks we had one, a money box. I'd learned from Melvin it was old country tradition to place cash and gifts with the dead to satisfy the spirits. I'd seen a few overeager families stuffing bodies with thousands of dollars. They packed mouths full of twenties; they folded rigor-mortised hands around hundreds. Out of respect I never explained to them what they didn't need to know. That the retort was an elaborately designed, computerized machine that recycled cinerary vapor through a series of funnels, and in the end, the only thing left was heat, not smoke. All that cash was incinerated over and over, and what remained was an imperceptible translucent streak shimmering from the chimney.

The retort's glow colored Melvin's pupils gold. He stepped behind the control panel and said, "How'd he die?"

"Car crash, it says."

Melvin said, "Well, help me carry him home."

I was working on a bubble. I blew it, and gum bonded to my upper lip.

Melvin tipped his head. "At what point did you get so weightless?" he asked, which was funny of Melvin, a funny thing to ask.

Each hundred pounds required an hour to incinerate. During the three days a week I worked, I'd discovered the job required a lot of standing around. Estimating from Mr. Yoo's weight, I thought he was an hour and a half, give or take. At the end of a life, I'd come to realize, some of us are reduced to six pounds of gray powder with two bored men pacing around our processed bones in a concrete room.

Earlier, on my drive to work, the sky had in it a purple tone I hadn't noticed before. I thought about replicating the crushed-grape color on an abandoned urn.

Melvin patted a boxy bulge over his heart. "Duty calls," he said.

"Mel, wait," I said. He pulled back the door. I said, "Did you feel that?"

"Oh, Mister Hilarious," Melvin said.

While Melvin stepped outside for a smoke, I removed acrylics, bowls, blotched towels, etc., from my footlocker and headed to the vault. The stairs to the basement were bordered by solemn cement walls that brought to mind a nuclear silo. The heavy steel door to the vault was open. Stepping inside, I smelled cinder. I briefly wondered whom I was breathing.

Newer burns were on the floor, stickered for delivery. These wood, stone, and bronze urns all had destinations: mortuaries, residences, a reserved spot on a flight to the Midwest. But it was the others that interested me. Lining a shelf along the back wall rested my blank templates, small cardboard tombs that held the remains of the unknown and the forgotten.

We had a contract with the county. Twice a week the coroner's minivan pulled up and rolled the bodies in. Some mornings, I'd arrive at work to find five or six horizontals already waiting. I'd also find Melvin, locked in the side room, talking to himself. Without names with which to invent a face, no birth dates, the bodies were mysteries. Our only clues were the coroner's forms, which listed causes of death. Suicides, mostly: gunshots, hangings, the filleted arms of the depressed. It was a transient city, and I figured these numbers were normative.

I was part of its transience, and I'd grown to appreciate the town's gaudy, burned-neck sensibility. Elementally it was a gambling town, what I considered a full-scale, interactive Dalí. We were practically cut off from the rest of the universe by a vast desert to the east and, to the west, a looming mountain range.

I'd relocated for reasons. The living was cheap, the sun shined three hundred days a year, and—it was becoming a pattern—yet another girlfriend had X-ed me from her life, a woman I believed I'd loved, who said in the course of our airless, tearless discussion that I'd always lacked ("was immune to" were Christine's words) emotional depth, which I just did not get.

In a few short months my hobby had transformed the vault into a lush underground island. I'd decorated nearly half of the indigent urns with a single impressionistic detail, whatever I could multiply from memory. An aspen leaf, a rivulet, green patches of forest. It was good for my mood; plus, Melvin liked it. He said my pastime showed real heart, unlike the delivery guy before me. Melvin had mentioned the guy had the habit of disappearing to the bathroom and communing with aluminum foil packets of crystal meth.

Melvin slammed the door upstairs and scraped around. Soon I heard low, sad strains from a radio.

On the far side of the vault, packed in a corner, were the paid-for castaways, an oak receptacle, a fancy cone-looking thing, etc.

Their only purpose now, it seemed, was to take up space. Looking at these urns, I always conjured up the image of a battered widow talking incoherently to a white wall. I'd think, I don't know why: here's what's left of a wife beater; here's the remains of a child molester. Someone had requested and paid for incineration. Someone had chosen a specific urn, but for whatever reason—malice, I suspected—the property went unclaimed.

The decision to use heat and light, a sixteen-hundred-degree oven, was an act of forced closure. And to erase almost all physical evidence of a person and abandon them to an underground cement vault struck me as . . . But it was just as well.

Delivering the dead was part-time and the pay was miserable, which made it perfect when going for broke. My move from New York had an attached aim. I wanted to earn less than thirteen grand by tax-filing season in order to qualify for subsidized housing.

Around town there were scores of government-sponsored apartment complexes—hovels, essentially, but they made ideal base camps. Cut-rate, no maintenance; it certainly wasn't a way to live forever. In any case, my time was largely spent outdoors, rustling inspiration from desolation. I was trained as a landscape painter, and desert was fascinating study. Desert defined the limits of civilized space. It offered an unobtrusive canvas in which everyday matter diminished or enlarged in proportion to the day's light. (I discovered detail in its lack of; I found lines in its shapeless barrens.) Anyway, there were just too many painters in New York painting New York, so when Christine chopped me off at the knees, I finally decided to place art on the top shelf of my life. But subsidized eligibility required poverty.

There were ample famine-level listings in the local Help-Wanteds—dish washer, lawn mower, etc. One ad, however, grabbed my attention. My reason for applying? I liked the gothic typeface on the name "Sunset View." I was also intrigued by the miniature logo, what appeared to be a Ming vase with wings.

I arrived in my van. The crematorium was at the bottom of a bronze hill hidden under a spattering of ancient oaks and surrounded by the sprawling, sun-baked lawn of a cemetery.

The manager, a man named Peter, escorted me into his office. Peter was one of the unlucky ones. He had a deformed cranium. It appeared that at some early fetal stage his brain had shifted bone to the right side of his skull, spawning a remarkable protrusion.

I handed Peter a résumé. He shot me a look of naked surprise. He said, "Usually folks forget to bring a pen."

Peter began the interrogation. He asked me what it meant to graduate in fine arts? I told him I painted trees. For some reason, he winced.

Finally, Peter said, "What's your temperament when it comes to bullshit?"

"Excuse me?"

"Okay, all right, fine." He was beginning to look upset, and I tried to decipher the reason. "You have a car?" he asked.

I gestured out his window. He stole a sideward glance at my van parked in the lot. I'd painted fat, swollen cumulus clouds across the side.

"Understand this," Peter said. "Some are hard deliveries." He leaned back executively in his leather chair, lacing his fingers together. "Say you hand over an urn to a grieving wife and she smacks you across the face. Not your fault, clearly, we see all kinds, but what do you do?"

I was startled by the question, but I appreciated the fact he'd put it out there. "Nothing," I said, speaking the truth.

"Sure, okay, fine," Peter said.

Peter drove me around the grounds in a golf cart topped with a lemon yellow canopy. As he pointed things out, Peter kept his head tilted to the left, as if compensating for the bulge on the side opposite.

We stopped at the crematorium. Peter threw a manual in my lap, said I should know a few things. When we stepped inside, the retort was preheating. Peter looked around, growing pissed off again. He opened the door to a side room, and a short man was sitting in a metal chair. The man was covering his ears with his hands.

"That's Melvin."

Peter led me downstairs to the vault. When I saw the dull brown boxes, the wall of containers stacked like bricks, my first thought was: mine. I thought, as Peter rambled: all mine. It was in my nature to renovate. A gray room, a vacant wall, I saw potential.

He pointed at the shelf. "At the end of the year these get dumped in a common grave. Melvin usually performs an amateur ceremony," Peter said. "No one ever attends, obviously."

I stood back, examining my painted cube of liquid purple. I pictured my collection of colored vessels disappearing under a pile of copper dirt while Melvin held open a bible, speaking of nonexistent things. It was a disappointing thought.

Impermanence, as a notion, frightened me. I quietly clung to the belief, foolishly perhaps, that through art there was the slim possibility of a life beyond, a second life made eternal by the white light on a gallery wall. After all, who wanted their legacy to be an echo?

The skin beneath my fingernails was stained indigo from my work. I tossed my brush into a white salad bowl. A violet mist drifted through the water.

After a while, Melvin clambered down with a dolly, rattling my nerves with each stair.

"Mr. Yoo is cooling," Melvin said. Standing safely outside the door, he placed his hands on his hips and studied the newest addition. "Springer would like it," he said.

It required a day to dry, and I decided I liked it too. I considered painting the rest of the top shelf different moods of sky, creating atmosphere above the leaves, rivers, and hills.

Melvin quickly began packaging the urns marked for the day's delivery. Counting Edward Yoo, there were three mortuaries on my list, one house visit. We wrapped the urns in parchment and then placed each into a cardboard box with winged logos printed on the sides. Melvin, in a hurry, sealed boxes with packing tape. Whenever he visited the vault he moved with purpose. He worked decisively, guardedly, as though the vault's door was some sort of demarcation line that he'd crossed.

From a back pocket, I removed my list.

"It says on this one." I touched the box with the cherry-wood urn in it. "It says Choking, Nevada," I said to Melvin. "Where's that?"

Melvin looked distant. "I've heard of Maybe, California," he said.

We loaded my van and spread a map across the hot pavement. Melvin bent to inspect it and his finger traveled east, across dried lake beds, over old mining towns. Unbelievably, his finger kept moving, until at last it stopped four inches from where we were now crouched.

"That can't be right," I said.

"Looks that way, Julian."

"That's at least two hundred fifty miles across the desert," I said. And it was. Choking was a miniscule black crumb in the middle of the state.

"Who's the delivery?" Melvin asked.

"Ellis, Mary," I said, unsure why I'd said her name that way. "She was my age."

Delivering urns to residential addresses was not my favorite activity. Each time I jotted down a residence on the paperwork, I noted the cause of death, the date of birth. I wanted to know how much of a storm to expect on the drop-off. Early century dates, even midcentury, a '28, a '48, those never registered with the same impact as the occasional times I came across a birth year close to mine. "She was a thirty-year-old suicide," I said.

"A real shame," Melvin said. He stood up, and I heard his knee pop. "You'll be back late. Tonight, I guess. Me and Springer have a date with TV."

"Fantastic," I said.

"Bring your paints. Look at it that way. Make it an excursion." I said, "Christ."

"Lord's name in vain," Melvin said.

Midday, and the heat was punishing inside the van. I leaned over to the passenger side, where dozens of cassettes were scattered across the floor. A thrift shop near my studio sold the things for a nickel. I noticed that a Lynyrd Skynyrd had melted into a futuristic molten sculpture. I located the tape I was searching for, cranked it up.

Naturally, I tried not to think about it. That there was a grave-yard behind my seat. Some days there were eleven, twelve card-board boxes behind me, so to keep it manageable I invented opinions. Today, I wondered, did they like my painted van?

Mr. Yoo thought, yes.

Kids liked it too; they waved. Drivers honked. Then there were the tough guys, their car doors primed gray, who usually stared until a stoplight flashed green.

Mortuaries were easy drop-offs. I rang a bell, a door opened. A strict face stared out. The city was fifteen minutes anywhere via the freeway, and by early afternoon Mr. Yoo and two others had been safely transported.

With house calls it was typical for someone to break down. A small child once answered the door, saw the box that contained his father, screamed at me, and then darted upstairs. I'd developed a stock response when situations got tight. "Yeah, yeah, yeah," I'd say slowly, accompanied by a few head shakes. One elderly woman had led me inside, prepared Earl Grey tea, and wrapped my palm around a large tip. Thankfully, I'd never been assaulted, as Peter had warned, but when one woman answered her door holding a spatula, she proceeded to smack the cardboard box until I dropped it.

I fueled-up at Milo's, a Mini Mart I frequented. It was near the I-80 on-ramp, and I figured I'd kill an hour, wait while the heat let up. I slid open the van door and threw a Tijuana-bought blanket over the last box, that of Mary Ellis. There was a quick sting in my bottom lip as I reconsidered. I took her with me.

Aligned neatly along the front wall like chromium tombstones was a row of blinking Quartermania slots. I noticed that my stool at the end was empty. That particular machine had once paid me five Benjamins from candy-bar change. Following that single payout, my synapses were prone to light up whenever I'd sit for a pull or two. I turned two twenties into quarters, and Mary Ellis slid in by my feet.

Sitting on the next stool was a short, obese woman whose breasts hung low and met in her lap. I fed the hungry mouth five quarters, got nothing.

In terms of aesthetics, Milo's was antichic. Fishing gear was sold alongside up-all-night trucker tablets, and puffs of smoke drifted in DNA patterns from ashtrays situated between the other gamblers. In New York, sure, I gambled. A Knicks game, a friend's poker table, a few hundred lost, whatever. Christine detested it. She said the money should go toward "trips." But at Milo's, I figured, my gambling was justifiable; it was another way to pick up tax-free cash. At the casinos, anything over six hundred was reportable. They made you fill out forms.

The woman sitting on the adjacent stool startled me by talking. "You from here?" she asked me.

I wasn't in the habit of fraternizing while losing my money. I inserted another quarter, picturing small walruses hiding beneath her loose T-shirt.

I said, "Me?"

"Yeah, silly, you," she said. She tugged back her lever, and I glanced at her zipped-open fanny pack. From the look of her cache, she was wealthier than me.

I said, "Poughkeepsie, originally."

"What kind of name is that?" she said.

The woman kept talking, spending, burrowing into her pack.

It was incredible. My machine was loose. Seven dollars in quarters and in a single pull it paid out again: one hundred and fifty-two dollars on three lined-up strawberries and a peach.

I collected my winnings from the cashier and returned for Mary Ellis. I lifted her from the floor.

"Have you heard of a place called Choking?" I asked my gambling neighbor.

"Sure, nothing there," the woman said. She looked up and I was struck by a pair of mesmerizing emerald eyes. She said, "But yeah, I've heard of it. It's a ghost town."

Desert was notable for its sterility, which was terrific for rendering on canvas, but the infinite wasteland grew tiresome. I steered east until the last signs of civilization melted from my windows and new backdrops exposed themselves. Umber, mountainous slopes were pockmarked with a million dots of gnarled sage. And the heat, even in the late afternoon, was relentless.

I passed one, two, sixty monstrous eighteen-wheelers. With the windows down, the growl of their churning engines filled the van. A faint trace of pleasure came each time I trumped one of the beasts. I wondered what unimportant things they were hauling, growing more aware with each mile that their loads couldn't match the gravity of mine. For forty miles I tried placing the name. And finally it arrived: Charon, the gangster who required payment to cross the Styx. We do have our myths. The Greeks laid coins on the eyes of their dead while the Chinese bribed spirits.

I cycled through cassette tapes. Most I'd tossed in the back to clear space for Mary Ellis's box on the passenger seat. But when my music selection wore thin, there was nowhere to hide when my mind wanted to stumble over pebbles of memory. A still shot of Christine as she wrote poems; her long, delicate fingers; how she'd wanted children; how at times I missed her.

The sky turned the same purplish hue as earlier in the day. And the farther I drove the more frustrated I became by the skeletal figures of crooked power-line poles paralleling me. Eventually, after a few hours, a faded green sign directed me to a two-lane highway. All at once the landscape's canvas enlarged, lengthened, and I'd never felt more alone. The middle-of-nowhere town was seventy more miles down a flat, empty road.

The only thing my stereo picked up was a country station, old pity music drowned by static. As the miles on the marker signs ticked downward, the station's reception improved. A man's gravelly voice introduced a song. The crackle in his throat brought to mind the sound of sticks breaking. The song was Waylon Jennings, and I turned it up.

Approaching town, I noticed a drab, fenced-in, jail-like compound set off from the main highway down an ill-paved road. Above the compound hovered a two-hundred-foot radio tower.

Choking was a Xerox copy of images I'd only seen in history books. Four brick buildings were padlocked, boards nailed over their windows. I crept along with the address in my hand. The only places open, apparently, were an auto body shop, the United Church of Choking, and a Chinese restaurant, Wok Here.

I pulled over. Odd that there wasn't a road sign for Highway 6.5. Odder still was the matter that there was a highway halved and decimal-pointed.

I drove to the end of town, or what someone had once designated a town, and turned the van around. I didn't enjoy the thought of wasting my afternoon, guzzling sixty in gas, and getting lost.

From a pay phone in the auto shop's dirt lot, I called Melvin at the crematorium. After no answer, I tried Peter's office. I got his machine. I hung up when I heard his weird angry message. To the west, the sun was beginning to fall, and I noted the way the tips of hills darkened and turned the color of plums.

I walked toward the auto shop's open garage. A young guy in khaki overalls stepped from behind a demolished car propped up by tireless rims.

I said, "Highway 6.5?"

"You're on it," he said.

I tried to digest this. I was on Highway 6, not Highway 6.5. I gave the guy the address.

"Oh, that's back aways, maybe three miles," he said. "That radio tower you passed. Between here and the station is Highway 6.5."

Choking, I decided, was the right name for the place.

I backtracked and drove down the poorly paved road, stopping in front of a gate. A ten-foot chain-link fence topped with spirals of rusty razor wire encircled the small brick compound. I wondered who would want to break in. Perhaps someone didn't want to get out. Behind the building was a trailer, its paint peeling, and parked beside it was an older-model sports car, dents in its side.

I carried Mary Ellis to the gate and pushed a button on a box. Blinds in a window split into a sharp V as someone looked out.

A buzzer sounded.

Another buzzer was implanted in a black grill door. I was gradually beginning to feel that the cardboard box in my arms—Mary Ellis—was live ordnance.

The door swung open, and an unshaven man with a thick shock of white hair stepped onto the stoop. He was in his sixties, I guessed, with all-around stubble flecked by spots of red.

I said, "Mr. Ellis?"

He steadied his hand by holding it with the other. There was a shake in it. "What's this about?" he asked. I recognized his gravelly voice. He'd been talking to me through my radio.

I gave him my name. Softly, I told him where I was from.

Mr. Ellis responded by closing his eyes, laying two trembling fingers on both. After a moment, his eyes opened.

"That my daughter?" he said.

I told him, yes.

"Set her down right there, please," he said.

As requested, I placed Mary Ellis on the stoop. Then I thought about leaving, quickly. Mr. Ellis squinted over my shoulder, toward my van. I turned to leave, and Mr. Ellis said, "You thirsty, Julian? A drink?"

His trailer was sparsely furnished. Except for a few charred ovals crusted to the stove top, the place was immaculate. Sharp ammonia fumes clung to the air. Out on the stoop, I'd been somewhat afraid to decline his offer, considering. Hanging on the wall was a warped poster of a ranchero strumming a guitar.

I asked for water. Instead, Mr. Ellis filled two shot glasses with cheap vodka and handed me one. He leaned a shoulder against the refrigerator. With each sip, his lips pulled back and I saw gums.

"Ten years Mary's been gone," Mr. Ellis told me. "The first time she left, she was maybe nineteen. Ran away with an older man, Warren, used to drive limos, a real son of a bitch."

On the refrigerator, pegged by an ochre magnet, I saw a snapshot of a young family dressed in their Sunday best. The clothes were from a different decade, and there was a crease down the center of the photo. I recognized Mr. Ellis without the milk in his hair, but it was the girl beside him, and the woman next to her, who captured me. The girl looked to be in her early teens. Curtains of red hair framed her round, cherubic face.

"When I got that phone call and heard how it happened," Mr. Ellis said, "I thought about it, you know, the way people think about those things. Thinking about it now too." He sipped and I saw more gums. "Anyway, when I wired money I didn't expect this." He pointed his glass at me. "You."

I studied the photograph again, memorizing Mary's eyes. I wanted them to speak. An unexpected ache sealed my throat, and I coughed vodka back into my glass.

"Careful," Mr. Ellis said. He looked over my shoulder at his little home. I asked him what he thought about it, about Choking. "Quiet, you know, but I have my music," he said.

Standing next to her father, her face beaming, Mary had her hand wrapped around his arm. I wanted Mr. Ellis to mention the girl's mother, tell me about her, but he didn't.

Mr. Ellis said, "I can't accept that box, Julian. Or, what I mean is," he said, "I know Mary wouldn't have wanted to come back. There's nothing here she liked. I mean is, you can find Mary a decent resting place back in town, I hope?"

I told him about the common grave, the small informal ceremony.

"Let's do that," he said, and he drained his glass. I placed my vodka, unfinished, on the counter.

"Time to get back to the station, son," he said. "We're running dead air."

In front of the compound, I dug my key into the cardboard box and ripped away parchment paper. I handed the urn to Mr. Ellis.

"It's a nice color," he said.

I didn't have anything, so I said nothing.

One final time Mr. Ellis held his daughter, and I noticed, though I wasn't certain, a look of injury enter his eyes. If there were tears, they didn't come. Maybe ten years without her had bled the man dry.

Then, unexpectedly, Mr. Ellis smiled and handed me the urn. His fingers had lost their quiver. He took out an orange pill bottle and poured three white tablets into his steady palm. He shook out a few more until the bottle was empty.

"Care to join me?" he said.

The ache from a moment before busied itself into anger as I pictured the young red-haired girl in the picture standing beside this man. I couldn't move. I simply stared at him.

One by one, Mr. Ellis popped the pills into his mouth. It wasn't enough to do serious damage, just enough so that he wouldn't feel anything. He held the empty pill bottle with three fingers, as if he were pinching a shot glass. He moved the bottle to his lips. "To women," he said to me, winking, and he tipped his head back and swallowed. He pulled open the black grill door, and when it closed, I heard the snap of a lock.

In the van I sat listening to static, waiting for a song to play. A minute of silence turned into fifteen, and I reached for the ignition. Several miles down the road a grim voice crackled from my speakers. As I listened to Mr. Ellis set up a song, I thought of what Melvin had asked. When had I gotten so weightless?

What to do with the dead, what to do with Mary Ellis. Even though I liked my painted collection of boxes, it was painful to imagine Mary's urn tossed into the common grave with them. I listened until the station dissolved into atmospheric clicks. A few high beams illuminated the van, but otherwise we were alone, wordless. We drove.

Blackness filled the night sky, and I decided to exit the highway, driving until I found a dirt road, a quiet little piece of nowhere. A mile or so from pavement, I stopped the van. Brush scraped my knees, and the cherry wood felt slick and cold against my fingers.

Although there was little to see within the void, I knew we were surrounded by sand, by granite rock, by mountains that had ground down into a sea of sharp, beige grains. Perhaps in another thousand years, I thought, there would be water here again, a sea, a lake.

I poured Mary into a mound at my feet. Deduct what I'd spent on gas, and ninety dollars was all that remained of my slot winnings. I knew it wasn't much, but it was what I could offer. I returned from the van with the fiery eye of my cigarette lighter, and the seven tattered bills burned swiftly on top of her ashes.

A warm space opened in the blackness, as gray strings of smoke drifted upward, and I hoped it carried Mary. I hoped to deliver her safely. The fire died out, a perfect emptiness descended, and I looked up, watching pieces of feathery ash vanish into a sky pulsing with fragments of white light.

Sheets

When Billy said he was leaving me for the Venezuelan, I panicked and took off for my hometown, Reno. It was a stifling July drive in the small Honda. I kept the windows rolled up, the AC turned off. I was trying to bake his scent into the upholstery, trying to season the car with the faint trace he'd left in it. Billy smelled acutely mineral, earthy, like a warm granite rock. I did not want to forget.

The first thing, in Reno, I stopped at Tiffany's Treats for a quick look. I subscribed to the theory that misery was proportional to, if not greater than, its cause. It seemed the thing to do.

I wandered down an aisle filled with scented gels and strip board-games. As I drifted toward the private booths in the back, the smell of bleach grew more evident. Apparently Tuesday afternoons were slow, as I was the only customer. Behind the glass counter stood an elderly man stooped over a magazine.

I found the wall with my videos. It was disappointing to see only eight lining the bottom shelf.

I picked up each, scanned the men on the covers, and read the poorly worded descriptions on the flip sides. As expected, the small collection was your average plotless nonsense sealed inside predictable motifs: the airline steward's first time, lonely nights at the fire station, etc. One box in particular commanded a second glance. It was an early eighties production, unquestionably tacky, but I liked the name: *Buck Goes Rodeo*. The young blond on the box (Buck, I assumed) looked exquisitely wholesome, in a Salt Lake City kind of way. A black cowboy hat tilted forward on his head, and slits in his leather chaps revealed strong thighs that ended in a pyramid at his crotch, which was covered by teeny bikini briefs.

I recalled once seeing my friend Frederick in a similar style of briefs, at the gym. He was a pleasant man but it was an unpleasant sight. I had summers off from the university, and my colleagues in the social sciences department, Frederick included, often teased me about being raised in Nevada, a state that continually rated highest in deviant variables. Alcoholism, high school dropouts, teen pregnancies, etc. At the annual faculty party, I'd discussed with Frederick my paper on social coping mechanisms. When studied at the micro level, they became highly individualized during crisis. I briefly wondered how Buck would rate in this analysis.

I strolled through the store some more, examining the sexualia. I considered buying a long roll of specially ribbed purple condoms. They had a few bars here, little out-of-the-way spots. I picked up a bottle of lube and studied the ingredients. The only compound I recognized was water.

It was my intention to keep my mind as far from South America as possible, away from the thought of subtropical accents. Tiffany's Treats seemed a logical diversion. I wanted containment. My Thursday psychoanalysis sessions would eventually foster acceptance, but I desperately wanted to skip the early stages of loss. I was terrified that if I stopped for a moment and let truth wander in, I'd be immobilized by the cold snap of rejection, followed by, for the third time in my life, the suffocating sensation of my heart melting into my lung. Once sentimentality set in, I was screwed.

I placed the video and a bottle of lube on the glass countertop. The elderly man's reading glasses had fallen forward on his nose, his full attention in his magazine. He traced a thin, wrinkled finger along a sentence. I noticed that he was reading about David Beckham in *GQ*. Measuring by his stoop and turkeylike jowls, I guessed the man was maybe seventy. He could have been eighty.

He looked up and said, "That do it?" He tipped his head, and his glasses slid back in place.

"For now," I said.

"Ah," the man said, picking up the video. "*Buck Goes Rodeo.*"

I never liked this part of the exchange: small talk. I stood with my wallet open, ready to give him the cash.

"Haven't seen this film in years," he went on. His mouth parted in a smile, revealing two missing teeth on the bottom. "Funny thing. The actor here who plays Buck, this I'm sure you don't know. Years ago he was the grand marshal of that gay rodeo they hold here in town."

Gauging by how he closed the sentence, he anticipated a response. I had nothing, save for the odd thought this man considered *Buck Goes Rodeo* a "film." I stroked my wallet, and after an awkward pause I said, "I did not know that."

My stepfather was on the couch, the television on. He nodded but didn't say anything when I came through the door. This was his way.

I walked past him on my inspection of the house, one room, the next, then another. I always roamed through the house upon return to see what my mother had moved. One year she'd swapped the family room with the living room. Six months later it was back again. She never explained it, only that this end table looked better over there. And once a vase or a chair moved, the entire room went with it. It was your typical three-bedroom tract house, mall-bought paintings on the walls, dark plywood cabinets, and I guessed my mother was trying to negate its overall sameness by lending it movement.

I went back to the family room, to my stepfather. Sunk into the couch, an anvil on a feather pillow, he was a lumberjack of a man. I could have drawn a mathematically perfect line from his eyes to the television. He'd worked roadside construction for twenty years, and the whites of his eyes were peppered with tiny cherries—permanent specks of red caused by flying debris, from not wearing protective goggles.

"Is Mom home?" I said.

My stepfather nodded toward the double doors that opened to the backyard. I didn't know if I was prepared to see her yet, my mother. While my stepfather was quiet, my mother talked nonstop. It was as if she were an appliance permanently plugged in to the wall. But her talking was the same as quiet, because nothing was ever really said. Sometimes I played along, but it was strenuous trying to fake interest in her gossip.

I climbed the stairs to the second floor. As much as I'd wished for it, my mother had never touched my room. As a consequence, it was a museum. I half-expected to find a plaque above the door, a wing dedicated to her only child. A corkboard displayed soccer medals next to pictures of friends I hadn't seen or heard from in years. Their faces were scarily young. The room depressed me.

I dropped my bag on the bed, locked the door, and inserted *Buck Goes Rodeo* into the old VCR. I needed distraction sooner rather than later. The television screen clicked to life, followed by the sizzle of static. I took refuge on the twin bed.

Like I'd hoped, it was marvelously antiquated. The first two men were hairy, meaty. One's hand over the other's chest was a claw, pawing. The set was a bedroom in a western bordello with coils of rope hanging from a four-poster bed and sheets spattered with lassos.

Buck's entrance was the next scene, in a field overlooking a cow pasture. He surveyed the muddy field, dressed in chaps, his strong white ass to the camera. A quick cut and we were back in the bordello watching Buck bathe in a wooden tub. The dark-haired man from the scene before knocked on the door, entered, and the pair quickly moved to the bed.

Tenderly, I ran fingers up my thigh. But something was off. I didn't know if it was the claustrophobic feeling of being in this room, watching this, but I was unable to focus. I couldn't summon a proper response.

Instead I saw sheets. The legs and arms of the actors only obstructed the view. Patterned sheets: squares of orange, brown, and avocado green. Sheets completely out of place in a western bordello; the colors were a specific time-place marker. I couldn't shake a haunted feeling blooming in my stomach. And to witness what Buck deposited on the sheets, what the other man rolled over onto.

I pulled back the covers on my twin bed. The sheets were a late eighties print, thick black and silver lines. Underneath the pillow was a mottled, ketchupy spot. I scratched it with a fingernail. It was permanent, a part of me, something I had left here. I wondered what had caused the stain. A nosebleed?

I threw the covers over the spot, stopped the video, and pulled out my cell phone.

"This is Julie," Julie said.

"Julie, I'm here," I said.

"You came?" Julie said. There was a cute spike in her voice.

"I don't know why."

"But I'm glad," she said. "Where is 'here'?"

"My old room."

"Oh my god," Julie said. "Stay put. I'll ditch work and come pick you up."

I'd known Julie since we were ten, in the fifth grade, several centuries ago, it seemed. With an unused master's degree in Russian literature, she now worked for a large casino. According to her business card, she was the "Senior Customer Relations Representative," whatever that entailed. The casino's motif was ancient Greece, but the last time I visited her at work, I could tell few people were impressed by Poseidon's fountain in Zeus's Sportsbook and Lounge.

While I waited, I went through old records, fanning them out on the floor. The more I examined them, the more the memories began to pile. I picked up a forty-five, remembering it as one of my favorites. "He's So Fine" by the Chiffons.

As teenagers, Julie and I would sit in this room during long,

hot summer days, painted in sweat, listening to these artifacts. Cross-legged on the floor, staring intensely at each other,
we'd whisper out bombshells, our mouths busy with secrets
and gossip. I remembered the distinct impression of feeling im-
mense, as though we were trading national secrets. It wasn't
long before we developed into normal teenage criminals. The
dealer was a friend of mine, a member of the tennis team. Julie
would drive, and we'd walk along desert roads after swallowing dry mushroom lumps, waiting for rocks to begin pulsing at
our feet.

I placed the Chiffons' forty-five through the turntable spoke
and the song began, which prompted a memory, long buried,
to surface. I rifled through the bottom drawer of my old maple
desk. Underneath a scientific calculator and, I couldn't believe it,
decades-old newspaper clippings, I located a bunched sock. I unfurled it, and out rolled an ancient sandwich bag. Mushrooms,
hardened to pellets and half-turned to dust.

A knock came at the door. I froze.

"Coleman? Are you in there? Coleman?" It was my mother.
The doorknob jiggled.

I slipped the bag into my pocket and unlocked the door. After a
light kiss to my cheek, my mother began.

"You'll *never* believe what's happened to JoRene," she said, sitting on my bed. "You remember her? We used to go to Jazzercise
together?"

"I was seven," I said.

"Oh, you *remember*. She remembers *you*. Anyway, JoRene was
at the Hilton bowling last week, and you'll never guess who she
bumped into. Do you remember that Derek boy you played bas-
ketball with? Well, remember his mother?"

The only thing certain with my mother was the obvious way
she steered talk away from my personal life. My private life and
the men in it. She was gripped by a vibrating fear that I would
spring the subject on her. As a consequence, she talked, thereby
preemptively filling the space needed for an authentic exchange.
It took years of frustration and a hundred hours of psychotherapy
to arrive, finally, at acceptance.

I looked at my mother, on my bed, with affection: my mother,
a nervous little bird, chirping. The image soon vanished.

I tried the flip side to the Chiffons. As my mother continued to talk, I lifted the needle, putting it to the beginning of the record. I nodded along. I left my hand on the stereo and, with my thumb, incrementally turned the volume louder.

We went to Julie's new apartment. It was in a huge complex that brought to mind the endlessness of an army base. She had her own covered parking space. Julie commented on this more than once as we maneuvered through the manicured walkways. She walked into her apartment ahead of me, her calm sway introducing me to the spacious living room.

"Well?" Julie said.

I stepped in behind her. Aqua wallpaper was plastered to the walls. Colorful little fish were swimming on it, forever stilled. And obviously the fun didn't just end in the living room. The hallway leading toward the kitchen was wallpapered too. I wasn't in the mood for this. I cut to the punch line. "This counts as insanity," I said. "You live in an aquarium, Julie."

"Oh, stop," Julie said. She slapped my arm lightly. "You should've seen the other woman's furniture."

Julie served whiskey. I clinked the ice around the glass with my finger as we quickly caught up to the present.

And then, inevitably, it began. I'd come home, she thought, to gain perspective. To remember what it was like before Billy: at the very least, to limit the hurt.

But, but, I said. The hurt had already set. I felt it in my legs, my lower back, and the dull throbs would intensify, I knew, as realization dawned. I'd come home because over the next few days Billy was moving out of our apartment. Now my apartment.

"Four *years*," I said to Julie. "And for what?" I went on. "A Latin with a flatter stomach? For *that*? We were supposed to get *married*, or recite vows, or whatever's legal this week."

"Breakups like this create a loneliness that feels close to shame," I told her. It reduced you. For months you were forced to occupy a two-dimensional body, as if everything about you, even your name, could easily be blacked out on a list.

Julie held me in her wet blue eyes, fingers laced in union, listening. But I had nothing more. There was little to say. There was only the whirring void in which to listen, like placing an ear against the universe and hearing, every once in a while, the stars clink against each other. I nipped from my glass as Julie twisted a silver ring on her finger. She did not have to say anything; with her gaze she reached inside, and held.

Eventually, after more whiskey, Julie unbuttoned her blouse, humming as she did so, and her blouse slipped down her body. Her salmon-colored nipples showed through the thin fabric of her bra. A roll of flesh hung over her tight jeans. She'd always been overly conscious of her weight, but I thought her curves were the prettiest thing about her. Looking at her, I felt frightened to realize she was the same girl I adored as a boy, but now, strangely, elongated. She twisted her black hair into a tight pony tail, revealing two turquoise earrings.

Julie moved to the couch and flung a leg over mine.

"I haven't shown you the bedroom," Julie said.

Her bedroom was undecorated, and it smelled of potpourri. Black tape was still affixed to her dresser drawers, securing them. I walked to her bed and pulled the comforter back.

"What are you doing?" Julie said.

The sheets were yellow meringue and looked crumpled, slept on. There was the vaguest outline of a body imprint on the sheets, and an anxious stir began whirlpooling around my stomach.

Julie was looking at me. "What?" she said.

"I don't know," I said. "I don't know. It's your sheets."

Julie was familiar with my brief bouts with the irrational. Nevertheless, she reached out and took my hand, interlacing her fingers in mine.

"There's always the floor," she said.

Sex between us was basic. On this occasion it was a vigorous, straightforward exercise in release. Julie used her mouth and I used my hands. It was pathetic, but I was somewhat frightened of women's genitalia; it was like losing an argument before the argument started. I was rusty with the workable parts. Still, I knew Julie's body well, well enough, and her orgasm arrived without complication.

Afterward, as we lay on our backs, I realized we'd been doing this for close to fifteen years, whenever neither of us was involved. Whenever, I realized, it was needed. I'd helped Julie during the James period—her psychotic ex-husband who still periodically called. His messages were menacing, punctuated with juvenile groveling, and I never wanted to find myself reduced to that.

I stared at the portion of her sheet that wrapped around the corner of the mattress. Now the yellow sheet bothered me only slightly. I pictured the quarter-sized scarlet splotch on my sheets at home, wondering. I had terrible ear infections as a child, and I remembered waking in the mornings with my cheek caked in blood.

Not surprisingly, Julie's bedroom was also wallpapered a bright, ludicrous aqua. It was quite exceptional, other people's tastes. My eyes drifted down the aqua wall. I paused on a tiny puncture made by a nail. A gift from the previous tenant, no doubt. I wondered how many punctures I'd left on the walls of my past, how many specks of myself I'd never know about, crumbs I'd never before considered.

Julie rolled to her side and slung her arm over my chest. She flicked at the hairs on my chest with her fingernails. She named each hair that she flicked after an ex, recounting each lover's key crime, cheating, lying, but to my ears they sounded more like Apostles: John, Matthew, James. Her breath was sweetened by alcohol. She said, "Let's be disgusting. Let's go buy stuff."

Sun Valley, I said. If shopping was the plan, I wanted to do it in Sun Valley.

"Why?" Julie said, scrunching her face. She leaned forward and began putting on socks.

I'd always been fascinated with the valley. Julie knew this, and I could tell it annoyed her. I argued my position as we dressed.

People claimed it was the largest mobile home encampment in the country, right on the border of Reno. Fifteen thousand mobile homes stretched out across the desert. As a child, I'd heard rumors about Satan worshiping in the hills out there, about a rock slab where teenage Satanists sacrificed stray dogs. The valley was transients and meth labs and not a lot of happiness. Many times I'd considered studying its population. I'd gather interviews, summarize the qualitative data, submit a paper. At the moment it seemed the only logical place on the planet to go shopping.

We drove to a strip mall Julie knew about. Two thrift stores sat side by side. Both looked nearly abandoned.

"Happy?" Julie said. She got out and locked the car.

In the Children's Leukemia Support store, Julie beelined for the men's suits. I browsed the books section. I was surprised to find a Steinbeck in hardback, the spine slightly water damaged, printed in 1961. A scribbled sign said hardbacks cost twenty-five cents, which gave me a scrap of joy. I dragged my thumb across the shelves hoping to unearth another treasure. Mostly I found self-help titles and poorly written contemporary thrillers.

I looked for Julie, who was across the store, wearing a brown suit over her clothes. She started modeling for me, turning on her heels, arms akimbo, striking poses. The pants sagged and the jacket made her shoulders look tiny.

I wandered to the back, to tables filled with junk people had bought and then abandoned. These were the things squeezed from people's lives to make room. I briefly considered the notion of material hierarchy as I picked up a homemade ceramic ashtray, a thin layer of film melted to the bottom. There were coffee mugs dotted with little chicken heads and dusty embroidered pillows. We never talked about it, but Julie and I understood many of these objects had come from the dead. I wondered what strange message they intended to pass down.

At the end of the aisle was a plastic garbage pail filled with bed sheets. The pail overflowed with them. They were bunched together, tossed in carelessly. I lifted the top sheet, but it was wrapped around another. It took a while to lay them all on the concrete floor. One set was emblazoned with a giant sailboat print, the mast extending from bottom to top. I unfurled a plaid flannel sheet, looking for sailboat pillow covers, and saw a long, black hair clinging to it.

Julie walked over, thumbs tucked in her belt. She'd added to her outfit. Now she wore a woven gardening hat and a bolo tie.

"I'm buying nothing," Julie said.

I studied the sailboat on the ground. I could tell the sheets were twin size, and would fit. "I'm taking these," I said.

"And *my* sheets bother you?" Julie said. "What? You want to buy underwear too?"

"No," I said. "Just the sheets."

––––––––

While I was out—I was gone a few hours—my mother had managed to shift the china cabinet and the dining room table. Once it had begun, the room would soon look entirely different. We sat down for dinner. My mother had prepared premade lasagna for the special occasion: her son was home. Because of my mother's reorganizing, my usual seat was now too close to the wall, allowing for only a few feet of space.

"I can't move," I said. I was sitting in what felt like a vice.

"It looks better this way," my mother said.

"But the person sitting in this chair won't be able to move," I said.

"The room's not done yet," she said. She landed an ugly glop of lasagna on my plate. "You wait and see when it's done."

My stepfather leaned back in his chair, appearing to stretch. He was listening to the television, which was still on, in the family room. I held a warm spot deep in my heart for my stepfather; the man, after all, knew what he wanted.

Later, we reconvened on the couch to watch more television. A vague sense of obligation kept me on the couch as my stepfather flipped through three hundred satellite channels. I felt myself growing hypnotized. My mother's talking was reduced to curt pleas as my stepfather clicked past shows that interested her.

"But that looks—" "Wait—" "Isn't that—"

Several times I attempted to engage my mother, but she was busy clutching my stepfather's elbow as he calmly, silently, sadistically held the remote control out in front of her.

As the channels flew by, I was reminded of Billy, reminded of the shows he enjoyed for their high camp value, usually whatever new teen drama was popular. Inevitably I'd grow bored by these shows, but I'd sit with him anyway and watch. I remembered once, attempting to divert his attention, I burrowed underneath the blanket, my cheek against his thigh, climbing his muscular leg with my teeth, moving upward slowly, steadily, until at last the television clicked off.

My stepfather finally settled on the outdoor hunting channel. He buried the remote control in the cushions to his left, out of my mother's reach. My mother studied the television. Finding little interest in it, she turned to me.

"Do you still see that girl, the girl you used to see?" she asked.

"Julie?" I said.

"Yes, Julie. She is such a nice girl."

"Woman, mother. And yes, Julie is a nice woman."

My mother began talking. I nodded in sync. For half an hour, through her talking, my stepfather and I watched as men clad in orange vests sat impossibly still in a tree perch, clutching rifles. The men were big, with fat callused hands—hands that screamed labor, fistfights, jackhammers. They waited patiently for a deer's antlers to materialize somewhere in the scrub below. When the deer finally appeared, the camera jumped and telescoped downward. My breathing grew shallow as we watched in anticipation. The deer's black eyes took in a leaf. In the perch, the men released excited pants, pausing for a clean shot. There was barely enough time to form a thought before one of the men ripped a hole through the deer's cranium, toppling it. Following this accomplishment, the hunters were pictured in a sequence of still shots: skinning the carcass, smiling, behaving like their versions of men.

Around midnight I brushed my teeth and stripped the covers off the bed. Three hours of watching television had left me exhausted.

I unrolled the sailboat sheets and smoothed them down. The boat enlarged when it was attached to a mattress; the sail spread full. For a moment I lingered on the comforting image of a small boy in the sheets, his mouth chalky with sleep, half-dreaming he was a pirate in a crow's nest, hailing the sight of land.

Records were scattered across the floor. I crept over them as I grabbed a piece of paper from the desk. I wanted to jot down notes for a syllabus, but the idea sank under its own weight. Planning always calmed me. A framed portrait of Maradona stared at me from the dresser. Soccer had once been my life; the sport had once consumed me—I missed being so devoted to something, so fully enamored.

Again, I thought of Billy. It was becoming impossible to filter out these appearances. His hands when they were cold, his clumsy body, his goddamn taste. After workouts his skin was charged, chemical; it was like touching my tongue to the end of a salty battery. On the desk next to Maradona's picture was a dyed rabbit's foot, which I now wished had brought more luck.

The nightmare was brilliantly vivid.

I awoke and the lamp was still on. I was dressed. I searched for my watch. It was nearing two A.M. In the dream my stepfather's eyes were slimy uncooked eggs. And in them floated little red blood-spots. And he talked; he talked quite a bit. About me, about my mother, about Billy. But as he talked, he blinked, and with each blink the yokes of his eyes began running down his face and into his mouth, until I could no longer hear his words through the wet, sticky garbling.

The tears came, uncontrollably. My chest convulsed with sobs. I felt an urgent need to vomit. I called Julie but she didn't answer. I thought of waking my mother, but that idea left me feeling more alone. The darkness of night brought with it acute terror, the feeling of desperation. I called Julie again. Nothing.

Slowly the panic ebbed, enough to allow in a moment of clarity. I shifted and felt a pull in my pocket, remembering. I removed the sandwich bag and rubbed the calcified mushrooms between my fingers. I hesitated. Then, in a sudden fit, I dug into the bag, trying not to chew, instead swallowing, as though I were a starved beast eating freeze-dried dirt clods. When I finished I coughed out a puff of dust.

My shoes were in the living room, so I found a pair of old slippers in the closet. The window slid open with ease. As I'd done as a boy, I stepped out onto the roof. The cool air bit into my face. I summoned enough childhood grace to shimmy down the side of the house, onto the fence, and from there to the ground.

I walked; I didn't know where. My mother and stepfather lived forty minutes by foot from downtown, the casinos. I headed in that direction until I hit a major intersection. The restless feeling of abandonment had eclipsed my exhaustion, and the spotted darkness only gave the feeling more totality.

In slippers I entered the first casino I reached, the Purple Coyote. A thick wall of cigarette smoke stung my sinuses as I passed through the revolving door. The casino's theme was Native American, and I was certain the designers hadn't given a second thought to being culturally sensitive when choosing its décor. An overweight woman whose thighs spilled over a stool dropped quarters into a slot machine fashioned into a tribal chief's head. The chief's bright feathers fanned outward and glowed, like those of a radioactive peacock.

I wandered around, over spiraled carpets, and soon realized I was lost. Mirrors pointed me down random paths, and I found myself directionless. I ducked inside a dark alcove, rubbing away tears that welled spontaneously. I called Julie again, but there was still no answer. Cocktail waitresses wore what amounted to one-piece tan swimsuits. Each had a swatch of leather over her forehead in order to appear squawlike.

I rested at a bar, straddling a horse saddle that stood in for a stool. The bartender served me a glass of water, and I sucked from a tiny red straw. The casino was mostly empty, yet the sound was overwhelming—high and tinny and nerve-wracking. Slot machines screamed at me. The ding of cowbells clanged from the opposite end of the gaming floor. I came across an elderly woman in a long nightgown standing hunched between two Chieftain slot machines. She fed the mouths of both, deliriously concentrating on eight spinning reels, looking as though she were on the verge of folding over. In the back of my mind, it became clear. She was being held up by hands that materialized from the floor.

I found a bank of elevators. I pushed buttons and rushed upward to a middle floor. There was a cleaning cart in the middle of the hallway and three rooms with the doors open. I scanned the hall. There appeared to be no one around. I stepped inside room 632, went to the bathroom, and splashed water over my face. Even though I felt nothing from the mushrooms, when compared against memories of the soft hallucinations, the person in the mirror undulated like a pond's sad, pathetic wave.

The bed was a California king, the same size as in our apartment—my apartment. I stripped the comforter and threw it on the floor. I stared at the sheets. Bows and arrows floated on the surface, but I was after what lay beneath, invisible, entwined in the fibers.

How many people had slept here, on these sheets? Hundreds, perhaps? Thousands? The industrial laundry machines couldn't possibly remove all the debris left behind, the cells cast off.

Carrying the sheets, I walked down the hallway and heard a woman behind me speaking Spanish, which turned into clipped English. "Excuse, *Señor*. Excuse." The pitch of her voice grew steep. "*Excuse.*" I didn't look back, and soon the elevator doors swept closed. No one bothered to stop me as I walked through the casino and out the revolving door.

I had no concept of time passing, only the feeling of paralysis settling in my arms and legs. The sun was peeking over the mountains. Light filled my eyes. For a brief moment everything was completely calm—a measured pulse to the streets, dust suspended in the air. There was no traffic, no blinking lights, and no movement in the sky.

From across the street came the metallic rattle of a shopping cart, a homeless man, his cart packed indiscriminately with objects. I recognized a propane tank, a sunflower lawn ornament. The man was wearing a torn denim jacket with a bulky blue sweater tucked into his pants.

He stopped when he spotted something in the gutter. Bending, he waddled forward, a finger pointing the way. He crouched to inspect an orange pill bottle before placing it in his cart.

He aligned in the crosswalk opposite. The light turned green, and I stopped in the middle of the street, watching the man come, wanting him to come.

The dusty smell of the sheets, sheets pulverized with tears, saliva, and human particulate, produced in me a quivering brightness. I thought of the countless people with whom I'd left parts of myself, and in the transaction the people who had become a part of me, by breathing them, ingesting them.

As the man passed, his hands clutching the jiggling handle, he supplied a gentle but fatigued smile, and I was struck with the feeling of unity.

In my pocket my cell phone chimed three times. It stopped. A car approached and slowed, the driver honking at me in the middle of the street. The sheets were weightless in my arms, a tangled bundle of air. The driver honked, my phone started again. Julie, I knew. We were not alone.

Mr. Epstein
and the
Dealer

The dealer doesn't have a girlfriend, no kids, di-
vorced once with a restraining order stapled to it. He lives alone
in Nana's pink stucco house and mostly watches a lot of TV. Paint
peels from the orange walls in long fine stripes; when he walks
through the house he's reminded of candy canes. Over the past
decade his habit has enlarged to a pack and a half a day. Among
his problems he counts his back as his worst. A dull pain radiates
in waves down his lower lumbar and into his legs. Several times
a week, the dealer spreads a *Penthouse* across the kitchen counter, flips to the stories in the *Forum* section, and jerks off into a
waist-level, flip-top-lid Rubbermaid trash can. Nights, he's often
kept awake by thoughts of unpronounceable, German-sounding

diseases that attack without warning. This he dismisses as a consequence of work. A few close friends, he's tight with Ralph. They have beers. He finds that too many words in a big situation are a great deal useless. They have the habit of sitting in his stomach like hard little pebbles, grinding his troubles together. This year, as an early birthday present to himself, the dealer is considering buying a Kawasaki two-stroke, two-cylinder Jet Ski. Overall he is, he supposes, satisfied.

So inside of an hour the dealer finds himself discussing odds of this season's Diamondbacks, boots up on Mr. Epstein's La-Z-Boy, to then later kneeling over the toilet in the old man's bathroom, vomiting. A wad of toilet paper ends up looking like a dead corsage in his hand. It melts to pulp under the faucet. The dealer wipes his mouth and glances at the mirror—tired eyes, his breathing even. Boots still firmly on the ground.

"My Spanish is leaky," the dealer says, clicking the bathroom door shut. "And airport customs. I don't know. That worries me."

"I don't blame you," Mr. Epstein says from the kitchenette. "But you're resourceful down to your fingertips. Look at the business you created. And out of thin air."

When Mr. Epstein speaks, his dentures come together violently, a wet clacking the dealer has always found irritating. "You'll find a way," Epstein continues. "It's not a big load."

The dealer swirls these last words over with his tongue as Mr. Epstein fills the electric kettle and turns it on. *Not a big load.*

Shrunken by age, bald except for Velcro strips on the sides, the old man says, "Here. Grab a stool. Peppermint tea will help settle your stomach."

Mr. Epstein's apartment is a one-bedroom efficiency designed for seniors on the verge: handrails lining the walls, emergency call button, safety-trip electric burners. Mr. Epstein has ordered every available option; he leaves nothing to chance. The whole setup is ripe with anticipation, a preventative terror bubble. There's a phone to the security desk next to the bed, large red arrows high on the walls marking the exit.

The walls are flat cream and lined with scuffed rubber base-boards. The dealer takes note. He is standing on wall-to-wall, industrial-grade gray carpet, a tight-woven synthetic with a plastic base, for spills. He knows things. He once worked roofs on tract homes before starting in this business.

"I understand it's a significant errand," Mr. Epstein says. "Ultimately it's your decision. But I have no one else to ask."

It's not the asking that angers the dealer; it's the nature of the question, the responsibility attached to it.

Earlier, Epstein paced nervously around the small apartment as he outlined his tragedy and lobbed morbid percentages about tumors this size, this grade, this late in the game. Fidgeting with an emerald ring on his pinkie, he linked one ugly symptom to the next, unrolling a long chain of medical facts as invisible bombshells dropped all around the dealer. Never once did the old man look him in the eye, and when Epstein finally finished, he collapsed into a pile of embroidered pillows on the couch, released a muted fart, and seemed to wander off into space, considering his awards, which hung like ornaments along the wall, honorary-this, distinctions-with-that, a man of achievement and renown.

The pair sat quiet. From the glowing eye of the TV screen, Carlos Quentin tripled; the scoreboard ticked another RBI. Slowly, a switch turned to "on" inside the dealer's stomach, stiffening it into a fist. Breathlessly he ran to the bathroom, closed the door, and locked himself in—his decision, resentfully, made.

Monthly, the dealer drives over the border to Nogales, never once with a problem. What Mr. Epstein wants, he's tried before for different reasons altogether, but his pharmacist in Nogales couldn't deliver. Mr. Epstein tells him, yeah yeah, whatever, he came across an article in the "Science" section in the *New York Times.* "The situation is becoming increasingly relaxed in barrios outside Mexico City."

But the dealer was hearing whispers about it, too.

From the kitchenette the electric tea kettle spits its whistle. Mr. Epstein, with a hiccup of shakes, lifts the lid of a ceramic jar with thin pink fingers. He says to the dealer, "Macaroon?"

A few years now, he's been dealing at Sage Gardens Royal Commons Senior Living Community, Tucson's largest tiered residential village and, according to the brochure, "Our desert town's warmest." With corporate headquarters based in Chicago and fourteen other locations across the country, it's a publicly traded company with an average growth rate of 15 percent per year and grounds modeled after small college campuses. The logo is a saguaro cactus (all shadow and pitchfork) with a sun downing behind it. Recently, the dealer has begun giving the idea of investing serious thought.

For sixty thousand dollars up front, Nana entered the Yucca Senior Independent Living building when she was eighty-one. When a fatty deposit dislodged from an arterial wall in her heart, wandering like a nomad to her brain, it cut her oxygen supply off. She lost sight in both eyes and partial hearing in her left ear. They moved her to Cactus Grove, the assisted-living quarter.

"Consequently," the social worker tells the dealer, handing him an informational pamphlet, "when the time comes, *if* the time comes, your grandmother will graduate to Memory Meadow."

He shares responsibilities with his sister, Eileen. Tuesdays and Thursdays, Eileen wheels Nana through the central square, where they feed imported ducks in the newly dredged pond. Mondays and Wednesdays, he accompanies Nana to "Creativity with Gina" or "Sing-along with Patrick," usually some activity that lets him escape two or three times to grab a smoke.

Nowadays he's accustomed to platoons of soft, yellowing bodies moving in slow motion across wide lawns. Each visit is a humorous lesson in fashion, bright examples of how bodies can turn on themselves. All-around flab hangs from underarms like plastic grocery bags full of water.

Nana's supplemental insurance couldn't cover costs for her twelve different medications; expenses spilled over. He and Eileen were flooded with notices. Monthly payments climbed into the hundreds, accompanied by phone calls at night from collectors.

The dealer began hearing little murmurs, and so did Eileen. One afternoon he packed a ham and jalapeño sandwich and took a trip over the border. In one expedition to Nogales, they saved three hundred dollars in blood thinners, calcium supplements, and antianxiety meds.

Nana was always overtalkative, more now that she's blind; so, shelved between stories of lacing pasta with ketchup during the Depression and praise for her grandkids, she spread word of his trips. He reminded her to keep everything quiet while he figured out the legal issues, like him sitting in jail. Nevertheless, orders came in. Nana's neighbors with absentee sons and daughters summoned him to their efficiency apartments. His trips to Nogales increased. He bought a pager and quit the roofing business altogether.

A Marlboro red stitched between lips, undershirts stained from years of hard work under desert sun, and Wranglers cut-to-fit boots he once kicked a man in the neck with, he became the dealer.

Now the dealer sees birds in the old man's pupils, wings fluttering, searching for an answer to the question.

Mr. Epstein's hand tremors again, and he pushes a coffee mug across the counter. An "I-Love-NY" logo is screen-printed on its side, an apple instead of a heart.

"Then there's the nausea," Mr. Epstein says, dipping his tea bag, dipping. "Happens mostly at night. But it's the high-grade headaches that pound after. You ever suffered your way through a migraine?"

Between them on the counter, like a thousand-pound toxic fang, sits the old man's preprepared, Scotch-taped, thick packet: round-trip ticket to Mexico City, one night in a hotel, expenses paid with compensation.

It's a nice gesture, the dealer admits, compensation and expenses. But the dealer also admits that a dark, blunted part of him wants to send Mr. Epstein's eighty-seven-year-old shriveled potato face into the cream-colored wall behind him, get it over with. This is not customary in any business.

The dealer, perched on a stool, quietly sips his tea.

"Noise heightens," Mr. Epstein goes on. "Your vision becomes tunneled. Daytime and it's as if you're driving at night with someone's high beams in your rearview mirror. I had a friend. Jacob. I see what's next."

There is movement behind the dealer's eyes as he pinpoints a vision of the old man's younger brain. Like a clock, steely and precise, a calm swivel of the gears for each breath. He draws a mental image of Mr. Epstein forty years ago, sitting behind an oak desk at the university, fingers folding his bottom lip as he solves a boring mathematics equation spread across a gigantic blackboard. A smile spreads across this junior self's face.

"I talk and I talk, I know," Mr. Epstein says. "I mean to leave room for questions. Do you have any? Questions? One, at least? You haven't said a word," he says. "So?" he quickly adds, his lips holding the purse.

Purple bubbles of skin sag below Mr. Epstein's eyes, pink membranes glisten. The dealer studies the silver ring on the old man's pinkie. The emerald winks when light captures it just right. The dealer looks around the room, the handrails, the buttons, all the precautions the old man takes.

"You've certainly thought of everything," the dealer says, taking the plane ticket and dropping the envelope in his shirt pocket.

"You could say that," Mr. Epstein says. "Your grandmother is a real treasure around here. I'm just sorry I never met her other half," he says to the dealer. "I'm sure he was a good man."

Yeah, a good man. Bubba, he and Eileen called him.

For a fifty-dollar service charge, the dealer picks up scripts from crippled rheumatic fingers one day and hand-delivers the merchandise the next.

His pharmacist in Nogales overlooks scripts written by American doctors for a two-hundred-dollar tip each month. One problem, however: the pharmacist limits the dealer on the synthetic and opiate-based narcotics. "No lose my license," the pharmacist says, his palms always raised to a ramshackle ceiling with rebar jutting through. The meds come in metric doses, but the old folks figure it out. Not his problem. But he has begun to spot more than a few laminated conversion tables left on empty benches around Sage Gardens.

Viagra. The dealer imports across international lines a tonnage of Viagra. He brings in Fosamax for osteoporosis, Dilantin for seizures, Aricept for Alzheimer's, Parlodel for Parkinson's, antibiotics, antidepressants, antipsychotics, blood pressure agents, uppers to wake, downers to sleep, megafiber tablets to shit.

He has a hollowed-out compartment in the bed liner of his pickup. He knows the border agents, and they know his blue Ford. Juan believes he drives down for cheap Mexican *putas*. John sees his smiling face on return and thinks he indulged in just that.

Recently, a family member approached him as he was walking rounds. She was a big-bodied woman with the eyelashes of a seal, and she wore a long, thick sweater that contained a bulging gut beneath it. It must have been ninety-five degrees in the shade.

"I hear you bring back things," she said, followed by a whisper, "from Mexico. You know. *Prescriptions.*"

The dealer stood patiently, having heard these stirring renditions before.

"My mom, she was diagnosed with leukemia a few months ago," she said. "The medicine costs two hundred dollars a shot. Her name's Barb. Barbara Pike, she knows your grandmother. Do you think you could, you know, check next time you're down there? It's called Epogen."

The dealer had a vial in hand within the week.

Two trips per month, sixty-four clients. Folks pay in cash, take their little white bag, shut the door, and lock it three different ways.

Mr. Epstein was the first to invite him in, and he liked the old man from the beginning. A kind person, thin as a scarecrow, with the soft, sad eyes of a fish, he always dressed in sport coats no matter what the weather. Mr. Epstein met him on common ground, despite his diplomas. They bullshitted. Current events, baseball, women. He particularly liked what the old man once offered about women as they sat around killing the last of Epstein's coffee.

"If she hates her father . . . if she gets that wild, nasty, terrified glaze when she talks about her father, run. Exit through the back door. *Leave.* Because believe me, no matter what you do you will inevitably become the living embodiment of the man she hates most."

Yeah, the dealer liked that a lot.

It's an early-morning flight to Mexico City, a nonevent. The dealer puddle-jumps to Phoenix before transferring to a larger plane. He crashes into a fitful sleep, wakes when the plane banks for landing.

As the plane taxis on the runway, his latest book drops from his lap and wedges between the seats. Next to him a stumpy American woman eyes him suspiciously when he goes to dig it out.

"Men Who Love Bitches," she says, her voice crimped. "That's an interesting title."

He has just awoken, he is teary-eyed, in a foreign country, and he doesn't know what to say. So he says, "I have learned it's possible that I set up relationships to fail from the beginning."

He passes customs under a gigantic, swaying banner that hangs from the ceiling, *Bienvenido a la Ciudad de México*, and out through the exit he feels concussed. The terminal is a pulsating circus. People pour from every direction, behind cars, on mopeds, jaywalking, pulling street carts, each with a different purpose in life. A cigarette eases his stomach, but already he feels lost, a stranger without a compass.

He tells a taxi driver his needs.

"That neighborhood?" the driver says through split English, and with an upturned thumb he raises the price. They make an arrangement.

The dealer drifts through the ride, bug-eyed, feeling as though there's sand in his veins. The sky is iron gray and choked by smog, and every other minute extraterrestrial smells waft through the cracked window. He is piloted through a dense maze of cars, buildings, underpasses, overpasses, and, incredibly, more people. From the boulevards there arrive thick strains of music. Ranchera blends with hip-hop, then melts into freestyle accordion, and at one point, as the taxi stops for a light, he recognizes Whitney Houston's dying-pig squeal.

The dealer operates on will and adrenaline, partially out of a strange sense of duty, partially because it's business. Business, he tells himself. It is his first, last, failed attempt to disconnect.

Mr. Epstein reminds the dealer too much of Bubba, Nana's Bubba. The old man owns a similar sense of humor. His teary eyes bleed Bubba's same spot-on calm. And why do men of that generation insist on, whatever the season, the sport coat? It's also the way the old man carries himself, really. Like Bubba, a few more years and Mr. Epstein's posture would imitate a question mark, bent to find his center of gravity, his walk a burst of shuffles. The dealer would never tell a soul, even Ralph, how he thinks of this as *cute*.

The dealer rewinds Mr. Epstein's descriptions about glioblastoma multiforme tumors, pauses on its exact placement, fast-forwards through its symptoms, prognosis. "Inoperable" was the old man's word.

For a bright, sharp moment, the dealer imagines a tumor the size of a small fetus living inside the old man's head, wiggling among the circuitry. The face is a bruised, veiny blob, and it has sharp little teeth. With each passing second, the blob gnaws at memory, light, sound, everything the old man holds precious. The blob speaks squeakily; it says, "I know you. I am you."

Chills shiver up the dealer's thighs. Mr. Epstein must be terrified.

The taxi seat is sticky. Gripping his book to his lap, he forces his mind to open spaces. To Nana's house and the dying patch of lawn. A back door that opens onto a field of brush and dusty desert sun. He begins to ache for the blow-dryer feel on his out-slung arm through the window as he drives back roads. His routines, TV shows, jalapeños on a ham sandwich—dumb reminders of the minutiae that never seemed significant, or important, until now.

———————————

The barrio is a never-ending wilderness of heartbreak. Similar to the barrios of Tijuana, much larger than those of Nogales, it's a world beyond description. A hill in front of a hill in front of another larger hill stacked high with tin-can shacks, and connecting each tin can hang lifelines, webs of wires, words trickling from the outside.

A stab of repulsion pierces the dealer's lungs when he sees a fat young Mexican boy sitting against a pole and shoving a glob of dough into his mouth, grease just corroding his cheeks. The boy smiles, his gapped teeth caulked.

The taxi driver stops on a corner. With a flick of his index finger he directs the dealer toward a decrepit theater that houses the *farmacia*. Painted above a 1940s style ticket booth is the international white cross that, the dealer guesses, means drugs in any language. Bullet-proof glass has been installed to protect the young woman who sits inside. Large brown eyes illuminate a pretty young face.

"Morphine sulfate, *por favor*," the dealer says through the concave ticket slot. The woman's brown eyes are nonresponsive, caught inside a magazine.

He wraps knuckles against the thick glass, startling her. "*Sulfato de morfina*," he says again. "It's crystallized. Little crystals. If you don't have that I'll take MS Contin, in pill form, whatever. I need a lot." He folds his fingers like he's holding melons. "*Mucho*," he says convincingly, and from his pocket he takes out a handful of the bills Mr. Epstein gave him. He peels away twenties.

"*Me entiendes?*" he says, asking if she's getting any of this. He's nearly reached the end of his Spanish skills.

The young woman carefully folds the corner of a page in her magazine—something called *ArtForum*. "You're trembling," she comes out with, suddenly, and in English. "Are you okay? You're so pale."

The dealer pegged her as the quiet type. Instead, she goes on and on, a cascade of verbal diarrhea, thrilled by the opportunity to speak with him. Her near-perfect English echoes through the ticket slot where drugs are exchanged for cash. And the funny way she speaks, he learns from her babbling, is patterned after the "like arctic cold but quite pretty" Canadian city where she graduated in biochemistry, class of '99.

In a hotel room near the airport, the dealer sets up camp next to the toilet and empties his stomach into it. Although, stupidly, he ate at a street-vendor stand near the hotel, he knows the reason he's hunched up like a sick animal. It's a city cut up into opposites, a bit carnival, a good bit more desperation, and he's been sent to drag a hand through the gutter, grab a dirty handful of it, carry it back home.

He draws the shades, confronted at once with darkness. In bed, the dealer returns to his book. He tries reading, but his mind wanders to the pictures of Mr. Epstein's daughters that hover around the old man's apartment, Rebecca and Miriam, twins, who abandoned Tucson in favor of New York and Boston. Both are unusually striking, he admits, but with a little bit too much of that bitchy look. Angled urban haircuts frame smiles just oozing with self-satisfaction. Still, they are an extension of the old man, the part of him that will continue to do the laundry, buy the groceries, breathe. Then there's the mantel, dedicated to his wife, Effie, taken by pancreatic cancer last year.

Back inside his book, page 48, the dealer pauses at the end of a paragraph. He starts at the top, reads it again. He's jarred by its precision.

"Some men love the independent woman, yet within this admiration there is underlying repulsion and fear. The man with self-esteem issues feels threatened. He therefore seeks control through manipulation, coercion, dominance. Recognition of this trait is the first step in righting future relationships."

The book takes flight across the room.

In the dark of his mind, it is the sound of paper being torn. The dealer jerks awake from a nightmare in which Mr. Epstein's dentures fly from his mouth and land on the dealer's neck; words escape—*asshole, murderer*—then they begin biting through flesh, artery, bone. In the nightmare's cruel, blue brilliance, pain manifests as an itch.

The dealer puts on the light, scratches his legs, chest, his moist armpits. He lunges for his cigarettes in his jeans and considers a quick, relaxing j.o. session but then quickly reconsiders, thinking of it for the first time in a long time as a disgusting idea. He studies the cigarette's bright cherry in the reflection of the TV screen. Then he flips the television on, trying to find comfort somewhere within the static. He finds himself growing irritated by embryonic pangs of guilt and sadness that creep though his limbs and end as a contraction at the pit of his throat.

Later, sleepless, an hour before dawn, the dealer prepares a shower and steps into a swirl of steam. He hopes to feel contained. He hopes to somehow locate an enemy strength he thinks is required to help someone die.

He knows the laws; he knows the codes. According to the United States government, it is illegal to purchase and then transport undeclared goods across the border and into the country. When the transported goods happen to be narcotics, prescription or otherwise, this is smuggling, a federal crime, punishable by prison terms, fines, an immediate strum of the pause button.

In the hotel room, the dealer pours morphine sulfate crystals into a Ziploc sandwich bag and tapes it to his groin. He vomits a half cup of soupy bile one last time and leaves a ten-dollar bill on the nightstand for the maid.

The pass through customs in Phoenix is painless. He half-expects more of a pucker factor, at least an eight on a scale of ten (ten being the time he got drunk with his friend Ralph, and Ralph snuck off to the bedroom, retrieved a shotgun, and began discharging it inside the house), but the customs agent's handicap is flirting with men her approximate age. He recognizes a smile laced with the quiet desperation he associates with easy targets at bars. He also notices—which accounts for a percentage of this desperation—that the woman needs serious grillwork done to nearly all twenty-eight of her teeth. He lays both elbows on the counter, supplies a heavy smile, and passes along a card that declares his only item to be a Mexican quilt he bought for Nana.

His pickup rests somewhere inside section C-18. On his trek through the parking lot, he draws a small amount of pleasure from the fact that more drugs are taped to his ankle. Luckily, the pretty young pharmacist was able to locate a cheap bottle of Haldol for a friend of Nana's. He's been told the woman's grandson sees pink monkeys and almost nightly listens to harmonica symphonies inside his head.

When the dealer first heard the story of Maria Lopez, it left him with lips clamped, teeth clenched down on the tip of his tongue. It was typical, among those regressing into the childhood sunset years, to welcome stories of hope, embrace songs meant for kiddies, play games designed for the mentally incapacitated. For the dealer, however, the story had the opposite, cynicism-forming effect, because when he counted up the inaccuracies, tallied the stuff clearly left out, it didn't matter how many times the story went through the Sage Gardens gossip grinder or prettied itself up; it was still, essentially, in a manner of speaking, *horseshit*. Fed by equal amounts of awe and fascination, the story of Maria Lopez has now graduated to near legend. She's no longer around, and no one who presently lives at Sage Gardens knew her when she lived, but her memory is a presence as real as a hundred-foot monument.

The story, though it varies in degree from one mouth to the next, goes basically like this: one afternoon, Ms. Maria Lopez, of apartment 208, second floor of the Yucca building, was watering her plants and leading her everyday, serenely boring life when, suddenly, the tip of her front toe caught the lip of a rug, and Maria Lopez nosedived forward and crashed into her hobby table, instantly fracturing both hips. She landed in the middle of the living room, too far from a telephone, out of reach of the red emergency button on the wall.

Maria Lopez's hobby (as the story goes) was constructing miniature *pensiones* out of toothpicks, from the San Miguel de Allende of her youth. All around were scattered thousands of these prickly friends, and she in the middle of the nest. Maria Lopez was eighty-eight, her glaucoma was worsening, diabetes going on ten years, arthritis, incontinent, spotty memory, five children, nine grandchildren—a full life that could have ended there and formed a substantive, honorable, three-inch obituary.

Instead, Maria Lopez (supposedly) began gathering toothpicks, located the bottle of Elmer's glue (massive pain undulating through her midsection), and she began to do what she knew: she glued the toothpicks together. For six days—again, the story fluctuates here, and the dealer knows that over time the days of her captivity will grow in proportion to her myth—for six days Maria Lopez never stopped gluing. She waited for one section to dry before beginning again, until at last she'd made a staff seven feet long, long enough to reach the emergency call button, which she pressed, with purpose, and five minutes later she was saved.

Because of his nature, the quiet orneriness he's fostered along into manhood, the dealer doesn't buy one word of it. Really, he figures, that afternoon the old gal probably just pulled herself (pain and all) across the room to reach a broom or a mop—because what sane, suffering individual would spend six days not crying out, frozen inside a tantrum, not terrorized by tears?

Still, the story is there, hovering like a ghost and protecting its community with its message. Often it's on the tip of Nana's tongue and in the reminders from her friends in wheelchairs who tug at his sleeves.

The image he's made of Maria Lopez (black hair, three teeth, smells of old fruit) fades to black as the dealer pulls into Sage Gardens and kills the engine. Warm desert sun fills his eyes, and for a brief moment he wonders—at what point does the will to die outweigh the will to live? What does the scale look like for Mr. Epstein? As a mathematician, what's his percentage of fear versus hope? And when did *one equals zero* become an acceptable equation?

A divorce in his pocket, all the arguments he has with Eileen, the dealer's learned not to question too much. He's come to understand that not every heart beats the same.

The dealer spends a few hours with Nana describing the progress of the shed he's put four sides on and reciting the specs of the Kawasaki Jet Ski she has, curiously, taken an interest in. But in his gut he understands that each breath and word and thought is only a means with which to buy more time. Eventually, when Nana insists on a nap, he walks the long route across the grounds to Mr. Epstein's building.

The old man, of course, is expecting him. Mr. Epstein stands bent in the yellow-lit open doorway, causing the dealer to wonder if the old man has eaten more than a macaroon since he left. They clasp hands briefly, and for the first time the dealer senses a shiver of warmth in it.

The dealer eases uncomfortably onto the La-Z-Boy and lays the white bag at his boots. Without so much as a word, Mr. Epstein hands him an envelope. The dealer quickly studies the cash and folds the stash into his jeans.

"You're a good man for this," Mr. Epstein says, the wet clacking present, as always. He relocates with a shuffle to the couch opposite and sews his fingers together. "Mexico City," the old man says. "It was warm. I mean, I read the weather in the *Times* and it said it was warm. So close, but funny I've never been."

The dealer is half-met with disbelief, as if the bag at his feet only contains an apple. The old man sure knows how to jump over topics.

"Tell me," Mr. Epstein says, "when you landed, what was the—"

"How will you do it?" the dealer says, impatient. He thrums fingers against the fabric of the chair.

Mr. Epstein's head falls back into pillows. Now, finally, a response. "Well, I'll make myself a milkshake," he says. "Chocolate, I'm thinking."

Of course. The dealer has rehearsed the process a hundred times in the last twenty-four hours. Sleeping pills followed by antinausea medication, to abate regurgitation. This is then chased by narcotics, the opiate-milkshake bomb.

"When?" the dealer says, and he digs a fingernail into his palm.

"Soon. Tonight," Mr. Epstein says. "I don't want to wait. What I mean to say is, I won't."

It's not what the dealer expects, and he doesn't know how to swallow this. Instead of a rush of sympathy, the dealer feels his face flush with anger. He imagined weeks, a few months from now, and receiving word during his rounds. His eyes would go vacant, he'd step outside for a smoke, ash falling at his boots as he reminisced. He'd call Ralph, tell him to meet at the bar.

For a moment the dealer has the idea of taking the bag and, hell, simply leaving. And then leaving this, now, for good. Maybe picking up a hammer again and roofing. On his walk over, the dealer began to quickly rationalize ways around it. He didn't know the old man that well, after all, not like family or anything, only the pieces of a man's life that have popped to the surface through all the denture clicking.

The dealer breathes in bursts, tries to contain a thought, one thought, but one is too heavy and it breaks apart. On the mantel, next to an eight-by-ten of Effie, the dealer sees a small stack of letters, stamped, orderly, waiting to be mailed.

Without too much thought put to it, the dealer says, "I'll stay."

Mr. Epstein's face washes with surprise. "But you can't," he says, clearly startled. "Laws in Arizona about this sort of thing are strict," he says. "You should know that."

"I'll take my chances," the dealer says, and slowly he flips the lever on the side and up go his boots on the La-Z-Boy. "I'm staying."

The dealer knows that Mr. Epstein knows the old man doesn't have a choice in this. Epstein brought him into this halfway up to his neck. And he's not about to leave, unresolved, and abandon a man—no, his friend—at a time like this. His exit through the black hole of that door will wait.

"Well," Mr. Epstein says. "I have no words."

"Words aren't always important," the dealer says.

"Right, right," Mr. Epstein says, nodding. "Well. Well. The game's on. I was just watching it. Watch the game with me?"

"Sure," the dealer says.

"Okay then," Mr. Epstein says. "I'll prepare everything later. After."

"Mr. Epstein," the dealer says. "Can I ask you something?"

"Why, naturally."

"You believe that story of Maria Lopez?"

As he balances with his arms and rises slowly from the couch, Mr. Epstein says, "Not in a million years," and he grunts.

A million years, the old man says. Years and years of living. It begins as a sharp, stabbing pain behind the dealer's eyes. The proximity to someone's death hastens the reality of his own.

The innings pass. Balls are snatched by gloves from the field; pop flies are stolen out of the air. There is nothing here but silence, thoughts blank of taste, and with them a weight begins to lift from the dealer's chest. He lights a Marlboro and feels a burn in his throat, a rhythm to his breath. He looks around the room, at the oak framed pictures, at the crystal knickknacks, the awards and the books and the keepsakes, at the stupid, silly things we leave when we go.

As night outside blackens the sky and Mr. Epstein's living room glows from a baseball game being played a thousand miles away in San Francisco, the dealer asks, "You think Bonds will ever get that World Series ring?"

"It's possible," Mr. Epstein says. "I'd like to think so. The man has a few years. A few more good years in him still."

Dan Buck

Vitus Hajek, the Czech, my greatest threat, trails by seven or eight miles, and in my ears there's the throb of a million hearts. Mile marker 135.

I run unaccompanied along a desolate stretch of America's loneliest highway, Nevada's I-50, which halves the state horizontally and now, at midday, at 101 degrees, ripples like waves of exhaust. The soles of my race flats leave gummy imprints on superheated pavement while a punishing sun reduces my vision to gauze. In the distance, I see only flat road, and beyond that a hallucinogenic dot where the road dissolves between two mountains. The finish line might as well be a cliff at the end of the world.

We are a group of twenty-eight. We are soldiers of the road, janissaries of conquest and pain. We are twenty-eight of the world's most hard-core long-distance runners, and by midnight, forty-two hours into the forty-eight-hour, two-hundred-mile Marathon de Sade, most of my opponents will faint, collapse into death crawls, and quit—their French, Bolivian, and Moroccan bodies depleted beyond reason.

I have paced myself in the middle by design. The key to a race is control. Always begin at the back; always lead from behind. I will overtake the rest after midnight, striking before dawn. My headlamp will spotlight a challenger's swaying ass within a blue-black backdrop. My strides will enlarge. I will engulf the ass, bury it behind me. I've been here before.

According to my doctor, right now a multilingual network fluent in adrenaline and endorphin argues among leukocytes, discussing whether I am experiencing euphoria or agony. My lungs are tight and airless. My will is serious as a knife.

But as epic as I know I am, I grow irritated by thoughts of the Czech who follows. There was a fight in the motel room several mornings ago, and my mind tunnels around the memory: Vitus's pouty frown, his bubble-wrap lips, the moping click-click of his argumentative tongue.

Over the past decade, I've cultivated the philosophy that 26.2 miles is for the weak, reserved for weekend amateurs and secretaries without a hobby. These "marathoners" lace up the latest pair of wave-technology, mall-bought Mizunos, safety-pin bibs to their chests, and, through jackhammer breaths, nearly die trying to qualify for Boston.

As I wrote in my best-selling memoir, *Über-Dan* (Simon & Schuster), "The entire spectacle is, if not a laugh riot, at least fairly cute."

Two years ago I ran Boston with a stress fracture in my foot. Each wobbly step shot lightning rods into my tibia and upward through my femur, terminating as nauseating spikes in my stomach. Still, I was able to jockey for twelfth position, just behind a wafer-thin Kenyan.

In the small, elite, insular world of ultradistance running, I lead the pack. Raised in rural Texas, thirty-three years old, six-foot-four with 3 percent body fat, I have a master's degree in molecular biology, legs that reach to China, and a smile born for heartbreak.

My face has graced the cover of *Runner's World* five times. Over the past several years, I've placed first, third, and first, respectively, at the Mojave Masochist 100, the Baja Six-Day Death Chase, and the Colorado 250 Coronary. The only superior runner I have named in print is that descendant of Greek gods, Yiannis Kouros, who blasted away 635 miles in six days.

I have been running so long that I know little else but the road. Each morning, at five A.M., I awake moving. Toes cracked, I shower, kill a pot of coffee, and destroy forty miles as a warm-up. I never cool down; I am relentlessly on.

I aim for perfection through mutilation. If it hurts, I make it hurt more. I strive for distance. I test how long my muscles can flex and release without disintegrating. I jog up to sixty, slam into the wall near eighty, break through at one hundred.

Nothing slows me. Nothing weighs on me. Nothing until now.

In this war, I stop for water every five miles and provisions at every twenty. The numbers count. My crew arrives hours beforehand to mine the course. The twenty-four-year-old twins, James and John, lash fluorescent orange grip tape around highway poles on the northern side of the road. I search for the stash hidden thirty feet beyond their marker, in the sagebrush. Time is maddeningly at stake.

I start my stopwatch, flip the latch on a huge camouflaged toolbox, and hurry. James, the prettier twin, has again forgotten the supersize Snickers. His aloofness is attractive, I admit, but disappointing. Instead of candy I throw a liter of water down my throat and follow up with twelve chocolate-chip cookies.

I slip from my shorts and jump into a pair of nylons cut at the knees. There's so much chafing between my thighs they look syphilitic. A former lover, now my trainer, discovered that L'eggs are perfectly designed for protection, absorption. A long-brimmed straw hat protects my face and neck. I reapply barbarian stripes of white zinc to my nose and beneath each eye. Hoping for a tan, I decide to go shirtless until the next twenty-mile stash.

Shoes peel from my feet like dead skin. From the kit I grab a razor blade. Its reflection smiles diamonds, and I slice diagonally across the volcanic surface of a blister on my heel, just below my Achilles. Dewdrops of puss form craters in the sand. I duct-tape the fucker's flapping mouth and quickly, pliers in hand, sucking carbohydrate gel from a tube, rip out a toenail that's turned completely black. Arousing shock-waves echo through my chest. I duct-tape the toe too.

It is 5:35. My Sportsman Timex flashes 99 degrees, 8 percent humidity. I have been resting for 6 minutes, 38 seconds.

For now, my appetite outpaces my nausea. Before heading to the road, tied into a fresh pair of Adidas, I devour a cylinder of CheezUms Pringles and wash the crumbs down with a Pepsi.

"Why do you run?" A weekend amateur asked this at a bookstore signing in La Jolla. The fortyish man, wearing a CLIF BAR T-shirt, was thin as asparagus. His bicycle shorts, sadly, left nothing to wonder about.

I told him, "Look. Read the book." I flipped to page 154 and pointed to paragraph 3: "What you're hoping for is pain so exquisite that all thought obliterates. Consciousness condenses into the seconds between breaths. You are reduced to soup made of blood and bone, an animalistic brew, and if you're lucky, within those breaths, between those seconds, and for a few lush moments of impermanence, you will be able to feel creation and the brutal transience of it, the instant of the Big Bang. You become, like me, godlike."

Sure, I'm that guy.

On a talk-radio show not long ago, I admitted as much to the host. That's me, jogging knees-high at crosswalks, spitting on cars that refuse to yield, ultimately lusting to reach empty roads where I can break free and race toward the hurt. The host fielded calls, which fomented confrontation from the listeners. I attacked the microphone for an hour, dissecting races, itemizing a laundry list of the hazards that can happen on the chase.

I've vomited boundlessly into gutters and bushes. More than once I've seized up mid-stride and blacked out, only to be resuscitated by the strange sensation of flesh ripping from my knee or elbow or face. Fevers have hit. Headaches? Shivers? I've endured outright convulsions. I've felt warm piss seeping down my legs. With no prompting I've laughed uncontrollably, whimpered like an infant, and after suffering through ten hours in the Chihuahuan desert, I went momentarily insane, believing I was witness to my soul peeling from my body, like skin from an onion. It ran out in front of me and I was unable to catch it.

What happened to Yury, the Belarusian from Minsk, is considered part of the gamble. Canada's Polar Paroxysm is a one-hundred-kilometer sprint through arctic tundra. Runners are considered triumphant not if they win but if they finish without losing a toe.

That spring day, surrounded by bright canopies of snow, I watched as the Belarusian, who was a quarter mile ahead, slowed. He pivoted and dropped face-forward like a felled tree. By the time I drew near, he was flailing on the frozen ground like a water-starved fish, pupils shoved to the back of his skull. Pink chunks of his cheek looked stapled into road-ice. There was nothing I could do. I relieved Yury of his camelback full of water, toggled the GPS on his necklace, and kept going.

Then there was last year, day four of the Baja Six-Day. My body lowered the drapes, and my vision dimmed. The Sea of Cortez rose and fell like an undulating bedsheet. Aquamarine knots tangled, vanished, appeared again, white caps bursting like blisters.

I was thirty miles past dehydration, and my sandpaper tongue pulsed against swollen lips as split as a dry lake bed. Dizzying by the minute, I loped along a cliff on Baja's East Cape, heading down a dirt road I hoped would eventually intersect San Jose del Cabo, which meant civilization and, more important, water. Out in the middle of it, the center of nowhere, I passed abandoned Mexican huts and watched the spray of a whale breaching a half mile from shore, which in my fatigue I interpreted as pornographic.

A drop of sweat swam into my eye; I blinked, and then there was nothing, just anomalous shapes of red and black. Thinking it would pass, I kept up my pace, stumbling over rocks, but when my vision didn't return I stopped, and I crouched, allowing my head to slump onto my arms.

What's interesting is that, even in exhaustion, you can still track your own delirious progression from sanity to insanity. You are able to understand you are plummeting, but you are completely powerless and under its spell. My mind was sliding down a bottomless trench, compressing inward into a thoughtless gray dot. During this eternity I grew comfortable with the idea of remaining on the dirt road, crouched into a pathetic ball, and never again moving. Also, I simply refused myself permission to push the button on my necklace.

Time passed as in a dream. Not far off a bell clanked. Somewhere between visions of waterfalls and the fossilized people of Pompeii, I felt a palm land on my shoulder. It slid to the middle of my back. Through two parched slits I recognized Vitus, the Czech runner. He was panting. Everything was tracery and blur. Slowly I began to comprehend that we were surrounded by a small herd of malnourished cattle.

Above me, Vitus grinned, flaunting his third-world smile. Quivering halos encircled his face. In clipped English, Vitus said, "This a funny way to die."

His crooked yellow teeth melted beneath serious lips, and with an eager grunt, Vitus lifted me from the ground, safely into his arms.

As outlined in the regulation manual, when a runner goes down, the search begins. A well-trained crew leader always has a finger itching to push the panic button. Before each race, cell phones are preprogrammed to summon EVAC helicopters and notify hospitals in nearby cities. Every runner wears the GPS necklace. When it's keyed to "on," teams trawl roadsides by van, searching for the blue blinking dot on their global-positioning monitors. Radio signals can locate a racer's altitude, longitude, and latitude within a tenth of a mile. And once pinpointed, the rescue web tightens:

hyperelectrostatic voices burst from walkie-talkies, vans careen, doors fly open, and fists pull the runner to safety. If you were a spectator, you'd think it was an emergency. Many times it is.

What's missing from the regulation manual is the mind-set of the runners. When an opponent does go down, there's the smell of blood in the air—alive with the wind, on the tip of each runner's tongue. Incisors sharpen and saliva gathers: another kill.

I spot a circus of lights illuminating the darkened desert road. I make my way toward them.

It's around ten in the evening when I pass Christopher Winters, the Floridian, one of a handful of Americans. His crew has him strapped to a gurney in the back of a van. Parked alongside it is an emergency vehicle. They have Christopher tubed intravenously, and he wears an oxygen mask. He looks more like an appliance than an athlete. Swirls of light paint Christopher's masked face yellow, underscoring his defeat.

I pause beside the van's open door. To test Christopher's spirit, I tilt my head to the left, gesturing, *Come on.* Christopher shoots forward, but he's held down by a swarm of hands.

Christopher has always been a close competitor, and briefly I think of taking the Marathon de Sade, taking the twelve-thousand-dollar paycheck, but more so, the title.

A mile or so from the commotion, I break stride and slow near a ditch. In the murk, I vomit bile onto my shins.

There is nothing to do on a run except think and not think. By now the movements of my body are mechanical. It's nearly computerized in its efficiency. To keep myself on the safe side of sane, I summon coping mechanisms.

In the past, I trained my breathing to synch with Wagner's *Ride of the Valkyries*, which began with a blast of snot from my nose, looped for ten or twenty miles, then died whenever I broke for water.

These days I'm bored with the song, with any song, and a book falls open in my mind. Chapter by chapter I revive passages of dialogue, visualizing scenes, characters, worlds far from mine. This year's choice is *Crime and Punishment.*

I am in an elderly woman's apartment when the twins interrupt Raskolnikov's misdeeds with five blasts from the van's horn. They race past. The van's headlights shine against a Wild Mustang road sign pimpled with buckshot, and for a moment I'm filled with pride. They speed toward the next supply point. Parallel poles of light disappear around a bend. I am cheered by their signal. They have given me the most up-to-date news on the number of runners eliminated. Five honks: five down.

But it's impossible not to wonder about Vitus—whether or not he's quit, or worse. I deliberate over this possibility. James and John would stop, right? They'd tell me. They've been drilled too many times. Vitus Hajek has a solid heart, resilient thighs, and the tenacity of a bull. Shivers course through me as I think about our talk in the motel room.

I make enemies with this scene for a few miles, creating fuel, but my irritation grates against my momentum, so I reintroduce Raskolnikov and discuss with myself his timeless predicament.

"It's all about the shoes," one lady said at another bookstore signing, this time in Seattle. "They tell me it's the shoes that matter," she went on. She was an obese lady with thighs that not only touched but made love.

I was surprised to find her at my reading, fraternizing with the usual crowd—vultures that toy with the idea of pain as sport. But for some reason, out of everyone, I respected this woman who wore skin-tight shorts and flaunted her rolls of belly fat as if boasting. Her dedication to maintaining such complete grotesqueness, and parading it to the world, was a kind of magic.

She continued. "So? Is it about the shoes?"

I signed her book with a fat-penned *Go Get 'Em* and said, "It's about heartbreak. It's about how cruel you can be."

Desert night is day inverse. Temperatures nosedive into the forties, and now there is blood in my urine. From the toolbox I douse my chest and back with lube to reduce friction. I slip into a long-sleeved breathable shirt. I am trapped in a slick cocoon. My headlamp bobs around the surrounding brush and draws a quiet response from a barren crowd.

I reload on liters of water. Water is now the third most important thing behind breathing, moving. Each cell fills like a deflated balloon.

From the highway there comes a noise. I freeze. It's the light rap of shoes against pavement and road pebbles. It's another runner. Another runner, approaching. I snap my headlamp off.

I move to the road and take position from behind, thinking it's the Australian, Billy Sharnella, lucky as always to make it this far. But when I see the runner's left toe drawing inward on the stride there's a snap in my chest: Vitus Hajek.

He's forty minutes ahead of schedule. Wondering how he closed the gap makes my throat constrict and my breathing skip its mark. Vitus wears earphones. He grips a dilapidated, Eastern European, war-torn CD player. Vitus and his talisman.

I catch Vitus by the shoulder. He reacts as though he's been electrocuted. He shrieks. His elbow slants high and hammers into the orbital bone above my eye. There's the sensation of dropping backward through space. I land hard on my ass and feel my nylons tear. The sky rips open with twice as many stars, and I feel a gelatinous bubble lowering over my eye, sealing it.

"Shit," I say to him. "Shit, Vitus."

I reach for my headlamp and light frames him, center stage.

"You frighten me," Vitus says.

"I *frightened* you?" I say. I am in shock. I am desperate to use words I know will wound him. "Dirty Slav," I say. I can tell, even from a short distance, the arrow lands. Arms crossed, Vitus turns away.

"You're so critical," he says. "So controlling."

"We're talking about this now?" I say. "In the middle of a race? In the middle of Nevada?"

"You're toxic," he says. "Like bleach."

"If you don't want to move in, move this relationship forward, okay, fine," I say. "But what about this?" I point to my pulsating eye.

"You frighten me," he says, retreating to his initial statement. Typical, sure, like always. "And I like the holding," he says. "But you like the holding too tight."

"Like I said. I'll try," I say. "I'll give cuddling a shot."

Vitus click-clicks his tongue and paces around me. He pushes a button on his watch. We both know it eats away at seconds being wasted. I make out two bloody flowers blooming on Vitus's white T-shirt, the source at each nipple. He forgot to lube up.

"*Kurva!*" Vitus curses. "I only try to run. *Ty curaku!*" Vitus snaps off his headlamp. In response, I turn off mine.

I search around in the nothingness and find nothing. Then Vitus does what he's so practiced at doing. He walks away, shoulders slumped, arms waterlogged, and for a moment I think he's left me. As I taught him during our training, if you can't win the race, you want the runner in front to shatter the record.

I turn on my light, and Vitus appears blocked by walls of black.

"Enough," he says. "No time more. We waste time. Okay, okay, I move in. Yes?" He kneels beside me. Quick fingers through my hair, he tastes like Salt Lake City.

"Be seeing you later," he says, standing. "At motel after I win," he adds. These words hurt almost more than any of it. My vision distends in triplicate.

"Wait," I say.

Vitus says, "What?"

"Hit me again?"

A black curtain in the night opens, and Vitus slips through it. I look down and see the glowing eye of my GPS pendant flickering. Vitus. The Czech. That dirty Slav. He pushed it. John and James will be turning feral about now.

One foot in front of the other, I lurch unevenly into a black blanket and up what feels like a hundred-foot wall. Through my one good eye, the broken yellow lines in the middle of the road bend and slither like snakes.

In front of me there's a highway, a dark desert, and millions of throbbing hearts. I can't tell, too early in the race, but I think Vitus just saved mine.

Mineral
and
Steel

"Tommy stole the goddamn Ford," my stepfather said when I finally answered. I'd been asleep, dreaming. Dallas's booming voice tore across my watery mind. He loved to harass my cell. "A pallet of titanium round bar, from the shop's dock, went *poof* along with the truck," he went on.

A hard exhale hit his phone, my ear. Refineries produced less smoke than Dallas.

Twelve-point Helvetica had blurred my vision. I blinked twice, but nothing in my trailer had enough edge on which to hang a thought. I'd been up late, pounding out four thousand words— chapter 18.

I said to Dallas, "Hold on. Who's Tommy?"

"One hell of an arc welder," he said. "He's been AWOL for days. So I need you in town like yesterday. Help me root out the truck. And the steel." He coughed up what sounded like a mouthful of phlegm. "I'll toss you some bills for helping," he added, which registered with me.

"This guy isn't coming back?" I said.

"Crystal meth's got him," Dallas said. "The shit's got Tommy by the hair hanging off his nut sack."

Dallas managed a twenty-man shop down in Washoe Valley. His business specialized in making door handles. He lathed, milled, polished, and shipped door handles all over the world. It had never been lost on me, sure. Dallas made an everyday object. A necessary object. But an object overlooked by everyone every day.

Since the small memorial service, we'd gotten together over a few awkward dinners, nothing special. As Mom's birthday approached, though, Dallas had begun phoning more frequently.

I said, "If I drive down, can we talk maybe?"

"You're breaking up," Dallas said. "I'm hearing electrostatic. Hello?"

Our connection hummed. But I knew he was avoiding, as usual. God forbid he ever discussed his feelings. His arterial bypass might rupture. We were numb, sure. Numb was honest. But I hated tiptoeing the line, wandering around the confusing, emotional demarcation zone that separated men of his generation from all that was demanded from men of mine.

A thin, shiny layer of condensation glistened on my sleeping bag.

"Leslie?" Dallas said.

I buried my hand in the wet. I said, "I'll be at the shop at noon."

"That-a-boy," Dallas said. I imagined a spurt of blood staining his lung.

If my mother hadn't married Dallas, I would never have spoken to the man. It wasn't complicated. In fact, it was simple: we would never have crossed paths. He and I were just opposite, frayed ends of a long, a very long, rope.

For months I'd been living up on the mountain, in Virginia City, Nevada, sleeping in a nine-by-five travel trailer. I'd bought the crappy trailer from a prehistoric woman in Reno, a woman whose smile was straight from a horror flick. Four jagged teeth poked from her lower jaw, and that was it. With this scary quartet, she chewed on her upper lip like a camel. When I stepped inside for a peek, the woman followed me, clipping my heels with slippers encrusted with kitty litter. The trailer was tiny, filthy.

I was now aware that even ninety-year-olds could rip you off. I'd paid nine hundred dollars, and a week later the door had become permanently jammed. I was reduced to shimmying in, and then back out, through a small side window.

Anyway, when I wasn't behind my laptop, I wasted plenty of time at the Bucket of Blood, a saloon popular for its heyday, Old West, shit-kicker vibe. Cracks wove through ancient floorboards, bronze foot rails lined the bar, and the spittoons were still used by customers with faded chaw-tin rings in their back pockets.

Autumn was sharpening into winter, which meant a slowdown in tourist foot-traffic. The Bucket's bartender, a bearded grizzly named Grant, was a rabid Oakland Raiders fan. Once a week he lit the place up with his twenty-eight-inch TV. Townies patronized the bar in the off-season. And game nights were great for people watching. (Wherever I went, I brought my moleskin notebook.) That bright, excruciating look of anticipation during Fourth Down and Inches made regular appearances. An Unintentional Face-mask turned Grant into a man bracing for a dump. But for the most part, customers mumbled away at one another, tipping back ice-cold long-necks, ignoring me as I ignored them. I was more comfortable sitting alone at the end of the bar, nursing hot tea, plucking stale pretzels from red plastic cups.

There was plenty of time on the mountain. Now and then, I went for hikes. The high-altitude desert air was waterless, and I enjoyed picking out unmanageable-looking peaks, then burning my quads on the rocky inclines. I knew to avoid certain areas. There was the slim chance I could fall to my death. Blankets of sage concealed small holes, deep gaps in the earth from former mine shafts. The tailings from the larger mines were unmistakable.

Tan-gray mounds, shaped like enormous anthills, decorated the mountain.

Virginia City, during its day, was a boomtown. The streets were terraced, alphabetical, and they cut into the mountainside horizontally. Everything in town overlooked the cemetery, a big, bald, desert hill topped with crumbling headstones.

D Street was once bordello territory, opium den country, and that's where I'd parked my trailer, in a dirt lot adjoining an empty clapboard house. The house was on the market. And one night I'd discovered, fortunately, free power. I'd run an orange extension cord through the back door and into a live outlet.

I'd come to the mountain to finish my novel. I'd worked on the book for years, tending to it like a garden—years of picking weeds, years of planting periods. Death had come. It had touched me. Death was the great reminder, and it gave me focus.

I wanted to resuscitate Mark Twain, to revive, through fiction, his frontier journalism days. Samuel Langhorne Clemens stepped into his pseudonym in Virginia City. One hundred thirty years separated us, but on the mountain, in my novel, he lived.

Within the span of three paragraphs, the town repopulated. Page 2, I shoved silver back into the gaping mines. At the newspapers, page 3, typesetters stroked letters made of marble. Silver rock ore was pulverized for its precious mineral at the stamp mills. An endless sun deepened wrinkles on the frowns of desperados. Most of all, flesh grew around old bone. That was the important part: resurrection. The dead lived again, they worried and cried and fought, they breathed, and so on.

I drove down through ochre-colored hills. The road was a winding ledge. Pink rock cliffs hung above me on one side. On the other was a heart-skipping drop-off. The city was forty minutes away by car.

Dallas, in blue jeans and a denim button-up, stood in the shop's open garage, rolling on the balls of his feet. A filterless cigarette dangled from his lips. With the unoccupied side of his mouth, he said, "Park over there, Leslie." And he pointed to a parking space with the cherry end of his cigarette. I considered running him over. Why he insisted on using my first name, I didn't know. I'd adopted my middle, Scott, years ago, after college.

I locked my two-door. "First question," I said. "Why are you missing titanium round bar? Who's ordering titanium door handles?"

"A broker out of LA faxed an invoice," Dallas said. He shrugged, apparently uninterested in the question. "Who knows and who cares. The paperwork said Dubai was the final destination."

My stepfather was a wiry man with small blue eyes and silver around his irises. Forty years of filterless Camels had rippled his face. I always liked to think his heavy lines were very late-Beckett. Hanging from his belt was a keychain, big as a hive, and he picked through it until he found his truck key.

We pulled onto the road, heading east. Dallas's truck tasted how an ashtray might. And its size convinced me he hated our planet. Burnt amber, it was a one-ton monster with a four-door extended cab.

Between our bucket seats, scattered among Dallas's shitty music selection—Elton John CDs, mostly—I noticed a used copy of *Huck Finn*. I'd given it to him as a gift. Bookmarking my stepfather's progress was a yellowing receipt. It hadn't budged.

I flipped the book to a random page. "Taking your time," I said.

"Like back in high school," Dallas said. "Me and books weren't meant for romance."

"It's one of the greats," I said.

"I'll take your word," Dallas said.

"Your loss," I said.

"Lots of that hanging around," Dallas said, squeezing the wheel. Inked in blue on his forearm was a Marine Corps globe and anchor. When he tensed, muscles in his arm made the world wiggle.

Elton John's obnoxious whine quietly bled through the speakers. I didn't recognize the song and I didn't care. Every pitch-perfect note was a torture device. I'd never understood why Dallas liked the pop star's music.

"So this truck thief," I said. "He's some kind of drug addict?"

"It's got Tommy good, yeah," Dallas said.

I said, "If he took one of the shop's trucks, why not file a police report?"

Dallas turned, somber-eyed, and he said, "Because Tommy's my best welder."

My stepfather hired these men, these ne'er-do-wells. Issues at the shop were continual. Whenever I'd hear about one, I'd imagine a line of fresh parolees stepping off Amtrak, desperate for work, their faces scarred by prison shanks. Dallas wasn't operating a monastery, sure. His line of work was shaping steel. Big fists were required for hard labor. These were men with muscled cables dancing inside thick necks.

His missing truck was a late nineties Ford F-150. That morning, on the toilet, Dallas informed me, he'd come up with a plan: we'd locate the truck, the titanium, and Tommy, all in one shot. But accomplishing these goals lacked any specifics. Not to mention, I couldn't point out an F-150 truck from an F-1,000. I decided on mentioning this.

At a stoplight, he gestured to another big truck. "Like that. But sky blue. With a dent in the side that looks like Italy." He went on, telling me to look for a bumper sticker with red lettering.

"It says 1994, Rock and Roll Hall of Fame, Elton John," Dallas told me.

"Naturally," I said.

We visited the scrap yards, sniffing out leads on the titanium. Any eager sellers drop by? Dallas fielded blank stares, followed by shrugs, and our plan soon changed.

"When Tommy tweaks, he likes to lose his money on two-dollar blackjack tables," Dallas said. "Let's dig around the casino lots."

At the Alamo, a massive truck stop with an annexed casino, we trawled acres of parking lot. Up one lane, down the next. The day was hot, and I thought I could feel a boredom-induced, constipating nugget form in my gut. Spending time with Dallas had never been high on my to-do list. My stepfather said little. And he smoked a lot.

When he reached for a fresh pack, ripping away cellophane with his teeth, I was waiting.

"Christ," I said. My window was lowered all the way. "It's a death sauna in here."

"Quit being a pussy," Dallas said.

"You want to drive around alone?" I said.

Searching my eyes, he moved his jaw roundly, as though he were chewing a horse bit.

Eventually, we pulled into a strip mall. He slammed his door. Puffs of smoke, like little thunderheads, gathered over him. A breeze from the east blew them away. He flipped his denim collar, tensing his shoulders to his ears.

A half-dozen parking lots later, there was still no sign of the F-150, the steel, or Tommy. Dallas drove us back to the shop.

"We'd have better luck if we split up," I said.

He returned my idea with a backhand. "Nope. I drive. You scout. That's the deal." To prevent any debate, he snatched money from his green Velcro wallet, folding five twenties into a square. He handed me his little sculpture.

"I appreciate the help while I'm working," I said.

"What do you mean while you're working?"

"I mean, while I'm writing," I said.

"Oh, that," Dallas said. He shook a cigarette loose from his pack, pinching it between his lips. "Yeah, well. Before we married, I made a promise to your mother."

My book lived on the mountain. I returned to it. I returned to Twain.

Twain had traveled west with his brother, Orion, secretary to the governor of the Nevada Territory. At first Twain tried working in a mill, then mining, and so on. When nothing panned out, he landed a newspaper job as an editor at the provincial *Territorial Enterprise*.

In 1859, a huge vein of silver nicknamed the Comstock Lode had been discovered beneath the town. It was directly inside the mountain. Half-a-billion dollars in bullion was excavated, helping build San Francisco and, later, fund Lincoln's Civil War.

My crazy mom. When I was a young kid, she'd plant my bony ass on the hump of her Harley. I'd cling to her tightly as we vibrated up the mountain. She loved Virginia City. The whole town was a museum, a skeleton with a heartbeat. She enjoyed walking along the elevated boardwalks, making fun of foreigners with cameras slung around their sunburned necks. The TV show *Bonanza* had popularized the place.

At the end of a day, when the sun began its descent, we would visit the bars and she'd sit for a glass or two. She liked the Bucket. She also liked the Delta. Mom liked to drink.

But before any whiskey nipping, any sending her son, fists full of quarters, off to the video games, we would lounge bar-side. At the Bucket's rectangular window, we'd watch smoldering sunsets set fire to clean desert ridgelines. Often, the gray headstones in the cemetery glowed yellow. Other times, depending on the cloud work, they looked bruised and purplish. Like every building in town, the Bucket had an excellent view of the cemetery. But like anywhere in Virginia City, everything kept its eyes on the dead.

———

Several mornings later, as I was inching out the side window, Dallas phoned. I fell. I landed on my back. As a rule, I didn't drink. As a rule, I sipped Darjeeling at the Bucket of Blood. I outlined paragraphs. I reviewed notes. But a game had been on TV. A bet had been placed, a glass poured.

I eased onto my elbows, taking inventory. A sinus thrummed over my eye, and my neck ached. My phone vibrated, indicating a new message.

I ignored Dallas's call.

Mornings on the mountain were quiet. Blanched by sunlight, the buildings in town looked ghostly. And the open sky was tremendous. Western skies reminded me why people bothered to pray.

In many ways, I was enjoying spending time away from Chicago, away from the urban syncopation of rush hour, all the headaches and lung-clogging pollution. Virginia City's fifteen hundred inhabitants were mountain dwellers—social awkwards, leave-me-alone types. And I liked to think I was starting to fit in. Each spring, townspeople hosted a Longest-Beard-of-the-Year contest. Grant, from the Bucket, owned the reigning blue ribbon, a bristly silver bush that hovered midchest.

But I had notes to take that morning. I had reasons to be here.

So I wandered downslope toward a historic mine. Liquidy visions of candlelit lanterns, hanging from poles, decorated a thriving boomtown that reassembled neatly inside my imagination. I listened for the past, for the dint of people cavorting inside saloons, the organ at Piper's Opera House, the cracking whips as quartz wagons hurried past.

Visitors could tour the mine for a five-dollar bill. Square set timber framed the mine's entrance, and trestle tracks were inlaid in the dirt, once used to haul out loads. Everything looked time-period appropriate.

The mine's original owner was a multimillionaire. Now a man named Wells ran it. I'd overheard gossip about Wells, how he rubbed motor oil into his overalls to appear authentic, to create mood, to bring in the tourists.

I threw back his tent's heavy canvas door.

"Do locals get a discount?" I asked him.

Wells's left eye was permanently bloodshot. It wept profusely. He was dabbing it with a red handkerchief. "Sorry, ten bucks," he said.

Ten bucks? Wells knew my face from the Bucket of Blood. I knew he'd seen me with his good eye, which now squinted hard at me.

"Tourist map says five," I said.

His squint toughened into a glare. This was something new. I'd never said word one to him. But I didn't want to argue. I paid him his ten.

Wells carried a thick candle. It threw white phantoms into the blackness ahead. The tunnel smelled of mildew. Moisture perspired from the walls. Near-rotten beams held up a dirt ceiling. Along the walls, huge rusted bolts affixed similar-looking planks. We walked for, I don't know, four Chicago blocks. The farther we went, the warmer it got.

The dark passage ended at the edge of a deep crevice. We were in a chamber of some kind. A cable hoist loomed over a bottomless hole.

"We call this here a slope," Wells said, suddenly adopting a rustic twang. He surprised me by turning the tour into amateur theater. As I was his only customer, he fast-forwarded through his performance, citing mining facts and peppering his sermon with "ain't" and "cuz" and "reckon," as though he'd stumbled into some Louis L'Amour novel.

Finally, Wells concluded his act. I peeked into the abyss and asked, "How far down?"

He said, "All the way, partner," and he blew out his candle. It was our only light source.

Total darkness made me a claustrophobic mess, and I froze.

"Not funny," I said.

I heard breathing.

We were so far under, so far in, it was difficult to envision a town or people or blue sky anywhere above us. Blackness could come quick for anyone. This I knew. The tunnel could collapse. In the flash of an eyeblink, we could tumble into hell.

Wells flicked on a flashlight. He casually handed me a pebble-sized piece of ore, telling me it was a keepsake. "And that concludes the grand tour," he said, and his voice normalized.

Another small tunnel branched off from our chamber. We were close to the cemetery. For a moment I thought about following the tunnel. I wondered if there were skulls and femurs set inside its dirt ceiling. Perhaps there would be enzyme imprints of bodies. Most likely, though, there would only be colorless dust, minerals, earth.

Outside, Wells's damaged eye filled with tears. My phone picked up its satellite signal, and it vibrated in my pocket. I checked the incoming number. Two new: both Dallas. Unbelievable. He was worse than a teenager with a crush.

Wells said, "You sit at the far end of the bar. You don't say a single goddamn word. You sit there and you scribble."

"I'm taking notes," I told him. "Writing."

"It's damn rude," Wells said. "When you're unapproachable, people invent ways to dislike you. It's our nature."

In Chicago, at the bars, you were anonymous. That was the point. On the mountain, the rules were different. Clearly, Wells believed he was owed some sort of apology.

It was still morning. My eyeballs were tender from the previous night. I was tired, and I hadn't slept well. I said to Wells, "My mom swallowed sixty-two pills. One pill, I guess, for every year she was alive. My stepdad thought she was napping. A hard day at work, you know? So he came home and he left her alone. He was scarfing a hamburger in the next room." I said, "He was watching an episode of *M*A*S*H* when she died."

Fright registered on Wells's face, and his eye began to flow. Then his face contorted into Pass Interference, and I knew our conversation had ended.

I said, through a crack in the truck's window, "Exactly what are we trying to prove?"

Dallas was pacing the shoulder of a four-lane surface street, stoking a cigarette. I'd kicked him out of his truck again. Rush-hour traffic whipped past. Wind rearranged his thinning hair into interesting, momentary hairdos. He paused by my window, sucking hard, saying nothing. Elton John was whinnying about love on the stereo. I shut him off.

Settling behind the wheel, Dallas said, "Twenty thou for the titanium discs is my estimate. Add in the F-150 and I'm out forty grand." He sighed. "Insurance will cover it. But I'm eating a fuck of a deductible."

"That's not what I asked," I said.

"You're the specialist, Leslie, so why don't you spell it out for me," he said.

I had given it a try. The night of Mom's small funeral, I'd tried talking to him. But he responded by bringing his wrist to his mouth, biting it, then hurrying from the room. Our loss was a massive crater, and it was only enlarging. Dallas loitered on one side. And I was on the other, waiting.

The hunt for the Ford F-150 continued. As expected, we didn't find it. No word from Tommy. And no titanium steel. There were thousands of similar-looking vehicles on the road. Still, we kept driving. I sensed that the truck was more than just a truck to Dallas. An acute desperation was growing within him.

After a while, Dallas said, "What's missing? Something's missing. It's quiet. Where's my music?"

"For the record," I said. "Rock and Roll Hall of Fame? Seriously? Elton John is not even rock."

Dallas blushed. "Sure he is."

"Not technically," I said.

"What about his song 'Crocodile *Rock*'?" he said, smiling, as though that cinched it.

One after another, we searched the remaining casino parking lots. We came up empty. Dallas made an executive decision. He declared that we'd begin looking around churches, grocery stores, malls, anywhere vehicles gathered. The dial at the gas pump turned and turned.

As we drove, as we searched, I thought about Tommy, this faceless, pathetic specter. Against the glare of the windshield, I watched short films, all starring Tommy. In the first, he joyfully sucked crystal meth through a hot glass pipe. This scene jumped to the next: copper wires, attached to a truck battery, affixed to his wrinkled ball sack. The film festival ended on the image of Tommy wearing paper slippers, dressed in an orange jumpsuit, jailed.

This would be my final run with Dallas, I decided. Enough driving around and looking for nothing. The end was near. Before my last period, my closing sentence, I was planning a daytrip to Berkeley. The University of California's Bancroft Library held Mark Twain's personal papers. He'd written his mother letters. I wanted to read those letters. I wanted to study them.

We were stopped, in neutral, idling.

Across a wide avenue, a new suburban mall lay like a distant mirage on the far side of a vast, hot, asphalt desert. The sun was falling behind the Sierras. I stared at the parking lot, thinking whoever had paved it was an asshole.

"We could always hit the range," Dallas said. "I renewed my membership."

He turned to me expectantly.

"Well?" he said.

"Nothing like bullets to brighten the mood," I said.

Targets and Tools sold drills and shovels and terra-cotta pots. But in the back of the cavernous warehouse was a firing range. Paper targets, screen-printed with animals, hung via wire in front of a bullet-riddled concrete wall. The wall looked vaguely war-torn. The size of your target, and your animal, depended upon skill.

Dallas threw his metallic briefcase onto a bench. He popped its locks. A sign instructed shooters to stand inside a white circle— AT ALL TIMES—when discharging weapons.

"A hundred bucks I nail the rabbit's throat," Dallas said, loudly. He was ready, preparing to fire. He was eye-goggled and ear-plugged.

"I can't match your bet," I said. But he couldn't hear me.

Dallas leveled his arm, cradling his right wrist inside his left palm. His eye slowly closed. If he missed, I'd get paid. If he made it, the cash was still mine. He made his shots. Then, as if to impress me more, he tore a hole through the rabbit's papery eye. I couldn't believe I was here.

I'd always considered myself a pacifist, left of things, and a little scared of firearms. But when Dallas shoved his .45 in my hand, adrenaline surged up my side, tickling my ribs. The Smith and Wesson was heavy, with a grip as smooth and cold as a watermelon. I took my place inside the circle. I imitated Dallas, taking deep breaths, closing an eye. My teeth chattered when I popped off my first round.

"Straighten your elbow," Dallas said.

I did. I fired. Then I fired again. One finger-twitch, I realized, could be harnessed into lightning. When my target was retrieved, Dallas and I stood over it, searching for punctures in the thin paper. Somehow I'd missed the entire buffalo.

The shop was dark by the time Dallas dropped me off. I was exhausted. Judging by the bags under his eyes, so was he. Dallas caught my shoulder as I was getting out.

"Huck's dad is a real shithead," he said.

"Pardon?" I said.

He picked up *The Adventures of Huckleberry Finn* from between our seats. He tapped the cover with his thumb. The receipt had moved, I noticed. It hadn't traveled much, half an inch maybe, but it was movement in the right direction.

"Twain owned a horse named Huckleberry," I said. "You know that? I mean, whatever. Never mind."

Dallas was searching for something, anything. He said, "It's fun. Huck's fun."

Fun, I thought. Then, I thought, *fun?*

"Huck is motherless," I said. "What fun."

It was an asshole comment, but I didn't care.

After a moment, Dallas said, "So we're going out again tomorrow, right?"

I didn't have the answer he wanted, the answer he needed. And what I needed he could never provide. Dallas understood trucks. He knew his guns and his steel. But the woman we had depended upon had vanished. And now we were stuck with the cold hard truth that neither of us could accept: we only had each other. So what did a truck matter?

Test results had confirmed the demon had returned, mutating out of remission. Mom had been through the nightmare once, and it had disassembled her. In a quiet part of her mind, she decided not to let the beast control her a second time. She wanted to dictate the rules. Every day, I resented her decision.

The anchor on Dallas's forearm moved. "You should visit her," he said.

"Visit what?" I said. His suggestion infuriated me. "A plaque stuck in the grass?" I said. "No thank you."

"I think you should at least—"

I said, "Shut up."

The writer enters an unspoken agreement when writing a novel. Clause number 1: few people will ever care. I read, I researched, I typed, years of typing, and no one cared whether or not I ever finished. Something was always on TV. Bread was burning in the oven. People were busy.

Still, by stringing sentences together, I hung my best decorations and hoped, eventually, someone would pay attention.

Literature had never made it onto Dallas's map of the world. I was sure that to him, writing meant not working, hanging out, participating in something *French*. I had 380 pages written. This was what I cared about—ink, pulp. And every single page was work. When he lived in Virginia City, Twain was twenty-eight years old, my age. My mother was dead at sixty-two. She would have cared, unconditionally. But she was busy turning into sluice, into dust, into mineral.

Even in early winter, the sun superheated the trailer. My miniscule home seemed too small for a hot plate, which in the mornings was littered with grains of mouse shit. In the afternoons, I napped. Nights ushered in an occasional nightmare.

When Dallas called, and he phoned constantly, I stopped answering. I wanted to be left alone. What I had to say to him frightened me.

I turned, as always, to Mark Twain.

His pseudonym originated from one of the two: 1) it signified *safe water*, appropriated from his Missouri riverboat days; 2) it was a shout to the barkeep, meaning pour up and mark down two drinks. Academics liked to claim the former. I liked the latter.

In February 1863, a dispatch from Carson City, Nevada, graced the *Territorial Enterprise*, signed, for the first time in print, *Yours Truly, Mark Twain*. It was the spark that ignited a wildfire.

During his time out west, it was common for journalists to commandeer extra print space. They wrote fake stories and hoaxes. They taunted colleagues and spurred on feuds. In the Nevada Territory, desperados were everywhere, especially at the local newspapers.

In one of Twain's bogus stories, he wrote about the curious discovery of a petrified man in the middle of the desert. Twain had a hard-on for the local coroner. He disliked him. And so his sketch of the perfectly preserved, winking corpse was an exact description, down to his wooden leg, of the coroner.

Now that was rock 'n' roll.

Twain's party buddy and fellow scribbler was a man named William Wright, a.k.a. Dan DeQuille (they loved their pseudonyms). My doorway into history was through "Tobias," William Wright's fictional "assistant." Around this trio I'd constructed your boilerplate literary thriller, commingling crime, history, and American letters. It was my hope that this decently written soup would someday spell best-seller. On more than a few sleepless nights, I became convinced that my manuscript was my only shot out of this trailer and off this mountain.

Dallas was crazy with his phoning. I nearly rubbed the decal off the erase button. Four, five times a day he'd ring. I'd envision his hangdog expression on the other end, shrouded by a cloud of smoke. I considered changing my number.

The weeks passed. I was knitting together the end of chapter 23. Twain and DeQuille were about to publicly name their suspect, a judge.

According to *Roughing It*, his hyperbolic "nonfiction" book about the West, Twain accidentally started a forest fire at Lake Tahoe. He survived blizzards and floods. He spun Quixote-sized myths. He was a world-class liar. That, after all, was every writer's job: lying. Only through lying could we ever approach universal truth. Reality was entirely too complicated to nail down. Fiction helped simplify the world, helped package it, give it a punch line, a moral, a meaning.

As "Mark Twain," Mark Twain could also act like a prick. One of his more notorious stories was that of a pioneer who massacred his nine children, "their brains dashed out with a club," along with killing his wife, whose bloody scalp he carried into town. The pioneer's life ended when he slit his own throat. The worst part? Readers believed Twain's fake story. It was reprinted in distant newspapers.

I finally answered my cell phone. Dallas's harassment necessitated a firm response. I said what I had to say.

"We are not related, Dallas. Remember that."

Dallas coughed into his phone. "So you and me, we wouldn't be friends, Leslie?" he said. "If it weren't for your mother?"

"I don't think so," I said. "I'm done with this," I said, and I hung up.

That night at the Bucket of Blood, I sipped tea and spoke to no one. By the look on the patrons' faces, everyone was preparing for a long, brutal mountain winter. I hoped that loneliness could be a decent enough friend.

I hiked to the top of the mountain one morning. It was thirty-eight degrees, and my kneecaps nearly froze. When I reached the peak, I rested on a boulder, taking in the town and the cemetery beyond.

I scribbled the name *Edgar Yuma* into my notebook. Shoving a forename against a city's, I'd realized, created interesting-sounding pseudonyms. The idea of *Leslie* on a book jacket made me nauseated. Other than swallowing sixty-two Dilaudids in a row, the only gigantic mistake my mother had ever made was the day she named me.

Jackrabbit shrub punctuated the landscape. When the wind blew right, when the sun tipped just so, their hard leaves twinkled across the mountain like tiny silver dollars. It was a reminder that the mountain was full of old jackpots.

Bobby Sacramento.

Twain left Virginia City in 1864. His star would soon turn supernova. The circumstances of his departure were typical of Twain. He'd challenged a fellow newspaperman, from the Virginia City *Union*, to a duel. Rather than being arrested—dueling was outlawed—Twain split for San Francisco.

Rock 'n' roll.

I awoke with a jaw-ache, as usual. My head was bouncing lightly on my pillow. Morning's light shifted in strange patterns through the side window, and where there once had been a clapboard house, the world was now in motion.

I slid open the window, saw that I was moving, saw that Dallas had hitched my trailer to his truck. Saw that Dallas was hauling me. My orange extension cord, which had ripped away from the empty house, writhed behind us like an angry tail, swatting pebbles on the road.

I speed-dialed Dallas. "What are you doing?"

"Seventy-two messages, according to my phone log," Dallas said. His voice was calm. "And you returned exactly none of them," he said.

I recognized Elton John in the background, ruining the world with one of his buoyant tragedies.

"Pull over!" I screamed.

Dallas hung up. My trailer swayed back and forth. It felt as though I were floating. I kicked the jammed door and fire shot up my calf. My toenail split from the impact. The cracked nail turned purple almost instantly.

I dialed again. "The police are coming," I said. I lied.

"Let them find us," he said. "Lots of trucks on these roads, as you know."

I leaned out the window, wind scratching my eyeballs, staring at Dallas's reflection in his side-view mirror. He noticed me. He joined in on the staring match.

"I finished that book," he said over the phone.

Given our current predicament, this information did not soothe me.

"Look, I'm trying to finish mine," I said. "Getting kidnapped doesn't help." I said, softer this time, "Please turn around, Dallas." He lit a cigarette inside his cab. A plume of smoke washed over his face, and he smiled.

Jumping out the window was impossible. The two-lane highway was a straight shot down the mountain, no stops. And Dallas was driving fast. My trailer moaned as it took a curve. I grabbed on to the kitchenette's tiny counter. The sound of sloshing urine came from the toilet's reservoir. I watched my laptop tumble to the floor. A piece of plastic broke off.

I blamed Dallas. He knew how I blamed him—for relaxing in his recliner, scratching his ass, watching TV, fifteen steps from my dying, overdosing mother. He might as well have driven me from my country, made me a refugee. Minus a mother was like existing without a guide map. I'd rather live without feet.

I considered the option of crawling out again. When we reached town, at the first stoplight, I could do it. But I knew I wouldn't. I would just wait. Dallas's little game would end. Then I would head back to the mountain. Maybe I'd settle down, grow a beard, learn to love the burn of whiskey.

I thought he was heading to his shop. But when Dallas merged onto the freeway, exiting where he shouldn't have exited, tectonic plates came together violently inside my chest. Narrow, winding lanes wove through the modern-looking cemetery. It was empty of headstones. It looked more like a golf course. My mother's resting place was plot 189-A.

Dallas stopped. Vases filled with lifeless, sun-scorched flowers dotted the endless lawn. Miniature American flags were stuck in the ground. I wasn't sure where she was buried. Her funeral was several hundred nightmares in the past. The graves, the rectangular markers, they all looked the same, all situated uniformly. I focused on a yellow patch of grass, a spot of dying lawn. That's where she'd be, the one causing trouble.

I stared at it. It was just it.

After some time, Dallas drove home, to the house. It was a bland four-bedroom trilevel tucked inside a seventies-era subdivision. He backed the trailer up the drive and onto the overgrown lawn, taking out a rosebush.

He walked the long way around. He cupped his hands and peered in the side window. His eyes were bright, an almost violent blue.

"Not on my goddamn watch," he said to me, and he turned, and he went into the house.

The outside world, more and more, was becoming an unwelcome place. I understood why people liked the mountain. Dreams lived there. The dead could breathe.

I remained in the trailer, reading, cleaning up, until nightfall. I watched Dallas's outline glide around the house, backlit by flashes off the television. A cheap poster of a young Twain was peeling from the trailer's wall. Dallas swept the drapes aside several times, looking out.

The night I'd returned from Chicago, Dallas was at the hospital signing forms. The house was dark and stilled. I'd pulled a queen-size sheet into the walk-in pantry and secured the door behind me. Facing my teenage bedroom was next to impossible. And hanging out in the living room was not an option. Everything in the house was poisoned: Mom's collection of shot glasses; a portrait of Mom on her bike in Sturgis, South Dakota. Every one of her belongings opened a fresh psychic gash.

The pantry was cool. I'd unfolded the sheet and lay down, jostling a twelve-pack of warm Coors. I wasn't, I'd never been, a fan of alcohol. But one by one, I'd finished them. At some point, in the middle of the night, I'd vomited onto a package of linguine.

When Dallas answered his phone, I said, "Anything worth it on TV?"

"Nothing, as usual," he said.

I was staring at the handle on the front door. It was simple, elegant. Dallas had crafted it from steel. He'd given it to my mother as an anniversary present. I was ashamed I'd never shown interest in the handle, two shafts arranged in a lattice, bulbed in the center, ending in a graceful curl like the tip of a flame. Everything steel was once iron, I thought. So it was conceivable, then, that everything iron was once blood.

I wanted nothing more than to be as useful as this door handle. Centuries from now, I hoped a few microscopic traces would remain. My blood could someday be helpful, a door handle, and why not?

Blood
Management

That night, Geoff found his young neighbor lying fetal on his sun-cracked driveway. The kid's spine was bowed, his knees drawn in to his chest. Geoff's white stretch Cadillac turned wide, fit nowhere, and now, as he came to a stop, its long butt obstructed the rest of the street. Headlights framed the kid in twin halos. His father's knives, Geoff thought—and now this.

Geoff honked, but the kid didn't budge.

Geoff knew this one by his harelip. When he'd first seen the deformity, Geoff thought it looked like a thick splotch of butter across the kid's forked upper lip. "Cesar" was the name he'd overheard from the others next door. All together he'd counted four of them—immigrants who'd come for broom-handle casino work.

Their rental was the same as his: two-bedroom, aluminum-sided tracts conjoined by a yard and, in the back, smashed up against a field of yellow weeds.

His new neighbors weren't typical twenty-year-olds, however. After the four had pulled up one day in a beat-up Mazda, they promptly weeded their yard and laid tracks of fresh sod. Then they bordered the green with roses. Not long after, Geoff had stepped outside one morning to find the youngest-looking one, Cesar, padding around on all fours, clipping away Geoff's dandelions.

"Hey, guy," Geoff said, now standing over the kid, Cesar. Geoff noticed that the kid's black, flaky eyelashes weren't natural, and he said, "Guy, what's what?"

The kid's face twitched, and his tong-lip quivered in a way Geoff thought wasn't right. Geoff didn't know what the kid could understand, but he said, "You going to stay like this all night? I need to park."

Cesar didn't respond. For a moment Geoff imagined two great cliffs, a deep crevice separating him from the boy.

Geoff said anyway, "You caked or something?"

After his neighbors had settled in, Geoff began quietly slipping out of his garage on late, lonely nights, when he'd crouch by the fence, thirsty for the comfort of voices. He'd listen to their high-pitched whispers. He'd hear the pop of bottles opening; he'd hear laughing. It wasn't in Geoff's nature to talk. His role, he believed, was as audience, as listener. As a chauffeur, listening brought in tips. Nights, Geoff's neighbors sat on their deck and listened to music with an accordion in it.

At last, Cesar managed to prop himself up by the elbows. He gently moaned, and Geoff saw that his boots were making dark tracks. He was standing in blood.

Turning the corner on his way home, Geoff had seen a black two-door racing away. Its lights were out and its rear tire jumped a curb.

The kid lifted his silky dress shirt, and the blood kept coming. Cesar's skin wept from a mangled smile just below his ribs.

Most mornings, Geoff stood in his kitchen, coffee steam melting from the window, and he watched one after the other buzz out the door like little hummingbirds, flitting off to jobs that required uniforms. He'd always thought the quartet made an interesting-looking family.

—————————

At the hospital, a nurse in a floral two-piece asked Geoff to spell his name. He gave her five letters, and she lowered her rectangular nose, penning them into the Family column on her form.

Past a door marked INTENSIVE CARE UNIT, down a white corridor, Cesar was resting after surgery to repair a stab wound. Geoff thought about the nurse's mistake, about correcting the family part, but nowadays he liked mistakes that went in that direction.

Anyway, Geoff's throat ached. His thirst was desperate. And he needed a quiet spot to fix. The loss of his father's knives had been fucking with his sugar for weeks. And standing around a hospital, he was sure, didn't help matters. When his sugar spiked, his thirst grew.

Geoff bent at a water fountain, thankful he'd remembered his gear.

"Bathroom?" he said to the nurse.

"Turn right when you reach the white hall," the nurse said.

All the halls were white.

Geoff instead came across a plaque that said Chapel. It was a simple, empty room, but there was something sinister at night about the dimmed, sunless stained glass on the ceiling. In the day, Geoff imagined folks tiptoeing over saints.

He sat in a pew, unzipped his kit. After pricking his pinkie, he wiped away a blood bubble. Then he fed the test strip into a battery-powered instrument. As expected, he was high. He filled a syringe, pinched a roll of abdominal fat, and buried the tip.

When Geoff returned to the desk, a police officer was busy flirting with the nurse. The officer drummed his fingers against his gun, appearing casual. Like some cowboy poseur, Geoff thought. Geoff overheard the cop talking about the "victim," Cesar, whom the officer called "wet-necked." The cop waited for the nurse's giggle to weaken. Then he followed up with what Geoff thought was a dark gesture, two fingers ringing an invisible bell. He did this with a limp wrist.

In the trunk of Geoff's limo was a Martin acoustic. A small-time country musician had forgotten it, he'd never called to claim it, and for a cool, hard moment Geoff daydreamed about lowering the twelve-string across the cop's neck.

Geoff cleared his sinuses to announce himself, and the cop said, "New State rules say we have to classify this one as a hate crime. But the kid won't talk—or can't," the cop said. The man had the open nose of a bull, which flared when he spoke. "A hospital employee from laundry is acting as translator. She asked the kid about family," Geoff was informed, and then, ending their little chat, the cop said, "The kid says you're it."

Nights, Geoff drove. Amid the bright, suffering streets, amid movement, Geoff tried to locate himself in a world where his parents had learned to die. With their faces stilled inside photographs clipped to his sun visor, their voices leaking from memory, Geoff was alone, continually wandering, a man in search of his place.

After carcinoma ate his mother, his father lost his grip. The disease first complicated his toes, next his legs, and finally his life. For thirty years Geoff's father had stood behind the lathe at Bob's machine shop. Metal shavings had pocked his goggled face. For Geoff's eighteenth, his father had given him a pair of handcrafted Bowies: two twelve-inch blades, ivory in the handles, gold hilts, and petite diamonds at the ends.

Nights, Geoff also had the habit of idling in the lot at Treasures, a shop downtown where Geoff had pawned these very knives.

Tonight, as he killed the lights, he counted the days. Less than a week remained before they'd be moved to the exhibit case. Geoff gripped the wheel. He felt nearly incapacitated by guilt. In the mirror, two dark blue half-moons were wedged underneath each eye.

Geoff had gotten thirty-two hundred dollars, cash, out of an appraised eight. Months he'd been falling behind in payments on the Cadillac. The bank was leaving threats on his machine. He'd tried shifting the burden by taking on preteen birthdays and high school dances. But after the hock, he was pinched again by 10 percent interest payments to keep his claim alive. Four point five grand—only that—would free them.

The day Geoff had surrendered the knives, he steered his Caddie to the Kitty Kat, a bunny ranch he visited to calm a sting that sometimes awoke inside his chest.

Ladies milled among shabby leather couches in the lounge, and Geoff was pleasantly surprised to stumble across Diane, an old girlfriend. He was aching for a bit of physical comfort. Diane still had the same blue veins running down her translucent temples. She told Geoff that, off and on, to supplement child care, she worked a room, and so they rolled around in it for a half hour. Geoff paid her in full even though she offered a discount.

Afterward, Diane slipped on white knee-highs with tassels down the sides. Then she gave Geoff the taxi story. Geoff, as usual, listened.

"You know, taxis are always late on clinic days," she said.

Diane made the introduction painless. The manager of the bunny ranch was a striking woman named Kitty. She dressed in a black suit. She invited Geoff into her lawyerly office and bolted the door behind them.

"Well, what *can't* I pass up?" Kitty said. The side of her lip rose in an inverted V, as though a hook had caught it. The lady was all business.

Geoff stuttered his offer. He punctuated the proposal with a reasonable estimate. Kitty's lip danced again, and she held out her hand.

In front of Treasures, Geoff stood before a darkened window, peering in. A neon sign blocked his view of the selling floor. Even so, he was able to make out the dumb, blank eyes of television screens situated along the back wall. The knives were here, somewhere.

It took Geoff a while to earn Kitty's trust. He won it by his punctuality. One afternoon, Kitty invited him into her office, as she sometimes did. She leaned casually against her desk, popped a mint in her mouth, and familiarized Geoff to "the notion"— the exact words she used, "the notion"—of telephone calling cards.

"Phones connect people via wires, Geoffrey," Kitty said to him, licking her bone-white teeth.

Mounted to the wall inside Treasures was a steel sword. Geoff also noticed an antique telephone, which dropped Geoff's mind on Kitty again, about their discussions, about the power of two voices connecting.

"Phones carry you to me, me to you," Kitty said to him in her office. "And people need people, isn't that right?" As he sat listening, Geoff soon gathered from her cryptic way of going about things that Kitty was talking about moving a large number of calling cards. Kitty wanted his help.

From behind, the jangle of keys startled him. Geoff turned and faced a roving security guard, a man with dough in his cheeks, standing with arms akimbo.

"Clearly, the sign says closed," the man said. He was dressed in a baby-blue shirt with a cheap badge pinned to the pocket.

"I'm waiting for my father," Geoff said.

And the man said, "Let's wait someplace else."

One crime, Geoff thought. He could manage it. One crime to save the knives. One crime to preserve the memory of a man who had fed his blood as Geoff fed his.

Elderly women, seat-belted, pushed themselves past him in wheelchairs.

Geoff was turned around, walking the wrong floor, the wrong wing. Maybe, he thought, the wrong life?

SKILLED NURSING, said a plastic green sign. Below it, etched in bold, ran a list.

The year is . . .

The month is . . .

The day is . . .

Madness sparkled brightly in one woman's eyes. She wore yellow velour, a black zipper down the middle. Her gaze was wondrous but disturbing. The image of a sickly baby bird came to mind, its head thrown back, its mouth wet with need.

He finally located the correct hall. The same nurse from before guided the way with an extended finger. She introduced Cesar's room as if parting an imaginary drape.

Large sunflowers poked from a plastic vase on an end table. Cesar was propped at an angle. He looked so tiny on the mechanical bed. One of Cesar's roommates was also visiting. The young kid wore snug white jeans, and he was caressing Cesar's hair when Geoff entered. He quickly drew his hand away.

"Hey, guy," Geoff said to Cesar, trying to find the words. Cesar's roommate grinned demurely, lowering his gaze. Silence descended like a curtain. Language was clearly a wall. With little to say, Geoff wished he'd brought a gift, a card, an offering.

After a while, the roommate squeezed Cesar's hand. "*Que te mejores,*" his roommate said before leaving.

Cesar lifted his one-piece for Geoff, showing off a square patch of gauze. The kid's belly was smooth, copper colored, with a thin crease of fat at the belly.

Cesar said, "*Me duele cuando respiro.*"

Geoff nodded along, and he said loudly, "You told that hospital translator I'm—what—family?" Geoff was ashamed by how his words entered the room, so thunderous, as though understanding necessitated volume.

There they sat, in silence, for close to an hour. At last, Geoff removed from his wallet a token from his meetings with Kitty. The phone card was good for seven hundred international minutes.

Geoff wondered whom Cesar counted as family. Part of him wanted to give the kid a hug. Instead, he stuck the phone card between two sunflower petals, and he left the room.

⸻

Occasionally, on his way to the Kitty Kat, Geoff spotted wild mustangs feeding in the hills. Once a week, he chauffeured the ladies to the clinic for chlamydia and gonorrhea checkups, every month for HIV.

A few miles past city limits, over the county border, he drove by sun-beaten quarry buildings, Wayne's Wrecker Service, and turned right at a dilapidated sign with a nude woman tipping a cowgirl hat. The bunny ranch mostly catered to excavation workers and interstate truckers who survived the hot, endless, open desert highways. Beyond a gated entrance was a clapboard building with three wings.

A bell rang when customers walked through the gate. The ladies lined up like marionettes in the lounge, half-asleep and wordless, a dawning look in their eyes, but when they saw it was only Geoff coming through the door, they floated to their rooms, gathered purses, and filed outside.

This morning, two tired tomcats leaned on the bar, softening themselves with Jim Beam. Geoff noticed Kitty, framed by her door, sipping coffee from a Styrofoam cup. She made her hand into a telephone and put it to her head. Geoff understood, and he nodded. Her batch of stolen telephone cards had arrived.

The eight ladies piled in and raised the Caddie's soundproof partition. It was the only time in their week when they were left completely alone, away from the eyes of men, and Geoff allowed them their busy-talk.

As he drove back toward city limits, the light on his phone blinked. He picked up.

"Geoff, can we stop for supplies?" one girl asked. "Nail polish?" This request was followed by, "Geoff, can we stop for burgers?"

Geoff figured, what these girls lived through, whatever the hell they wanted.

He dropped them at the clinic and went on his rounds, stopping by the casinos.

The Kitty Kat's menus were printed on thick, tan vellum, and they ball-parked prices and times. Fifteen minutes, a half hour, the prices rose accordingly. A convention weekend was coming up, which meant good business, so Geoff paper-clipped some of his business cards to a few of the menus.

Geoff knew Kitty liked his line of work. That's why he'd gotten the gig. Kitty read angles. She knew the kind of people he had to know in his business. Mostly, he knew valets, and knowing valets was worth something.

Geoff pulled in at the Purple Coyote, a four-hundred-room palace. Its gaming floor spread across twenty indoor acres. The Purple Coyote's head valet, a man named Michel, stepped out from a glass booth. Michel was of West Indian descent, and his sharp brown nose was as even as a blade. But that nose: it was a problem for Michel, from the money he shoveled into it.

Michel gestured to a quieter part of the covered driveway. Geoff followed.

"Let me say, I absolutely 100 percent hate talking here," Michel said. His eyes darted sideways, focusing again on Geoff. "But I chitchatted with my guys and it's not a problem. For five bucks per, we'll unload the cards to the migrants in kitchen and housekeeping." Michel rubbed his nostril with his thumb. Michel said, "How many are we talking?"

Geoff told him, for now, to keep the first package light: ten thousand.

Michel drew a breath, doing the math. Geoff handed Michel his bundle of menus for distribution. A fifty was paper-clipped to the one on top.

As usual, the ladies were lined up on the sidewalk in front of the clinic. Band-Aids with little hearts on them decorated the folds of their arms. The girl who'd asked about stopping for supplies liked the idea of favors. Tipping her head, she asked Geoff to drive by her mother's place. "Just to see," she said. And he obliged, noticing a new Honda in the drive.

Geoff's throat loosened, allowing in a breath laced with panic. He jerked awake. He'd been dreaming of the knives. He realized he'd been sobbing violently and biting his pillow as he slept. Tearstains darkened on his frayed, yellow sham in the shape of ants.

He had lain down for an afternoon nap. Now the sky was filled with a dying orange glow. His tongue was dry, rough as a dirt clod. Loneliness and money worries, he was sure, compounded his symptoms.

Geoff didn't bother with his blood in the bathroom. He didn't have the patience to stare at the numbers again. He tapped a syringe and shot a string of insulin-rich fluid into the air. After driving the spike in for the thousand-thousandth time, he showered.

When Geoff was given the news as a boy, his father's story was that he'd passed along a tiny creature, down through his genes, and it awoke inside Geoff when he was capable of feeding it. The trouble was, his father had fed his creature until it grew large enough to rip apart wiring. After his death, Geoff had stepped into his father's shoes, only to realize that filling them lacked any real purpose.

Geoff stood at the kitchen window, a wet towel draped around his hips. Because of its length, his Cadillac stuck ass-out from the garage. He was unable to completely lower the door. Without any clients tonight, he figured he'd just drive around, move through space, claim whatever his role was in it.

The sight of Cesar marching across his overgrown lawn, carrying a casserole dish, struck Geoff as odd. Cesar's hands were in pink oven mitts.

Geoff threw on pants, a T-shirt. He opened the door. Cesar was wearing an argyle button-up and his thick black hair was combed and parted. A tiny diamond glittered on his earlobe.

Cesar smirked. It was a unique, cruel mouth, but even so, Geoff drew a shiver of warmth from the way the boy's upper lip parted. A sting briefly entered Geoff's throat when he realized Cesar was that exact age—that if things in his life had turned out differently, the boy could have been his.

Geoff backed against the door. Cesar walked the casserole to the kitchen, where he began riffling through Geoff's drawers.

Geoff didn't own a single piece of dining room furniture. He used the room to store his weight bench. So Cesar set the coffee table instead. From his pocket, Cesar removed a small Spanish-English dictionary. He paged through it.

"Lasagna pasta," Cesar said. After more flipping, he said, "No bread. *Lo siento.*"

Gusts of peppermint wafted through the bright fluorescence of Kitty's office. She leaned back in her decision-making chair, clicking the end of a ballpoint pen. Her office was air-conditioned, spacious. Kitty opened a folder. In it was a log—names, numbers, what appeared to be a tree's worth of paper.

Kitty said to Geoff, "This package fell from the back of a truck, is what I'm saying." Kitty said, "And what I'm telling you is, you find these cards a home and we'll take care of your end." She said, "It's important you listen to what I'm saying."

A lunch pail–sized cardboard box with a familiar logo stamped on its side sat in the middle of Kitty's desk. Next to it was an emerald-encrusted ashtray. Because Kitty didn't smoke, it was ashless. It gleamed.

Later that morning, Geoff met his connection, Michel, the valet, at a furniture outlet store. Michel periodically tapped his nostril with the nub of his thumb. They wandered around prearranged model rooms in the middle of the large, cold warehouse.

Michel said, "Let me say, I appreciate you meeting me here this time."

They walked and Geoff listened, noting the number of times Michel's thumb visited his nose. Eventually, Geoff handed Michel his car keys.

Michel said, "Everything in your trunk?"

"Look inside the guitar case," Geoff said.

"I'll be back," Michel said. He gestured to a walnut bed frame. "Look around. I bought a nice dresser here last year."

As Geoff waited, he did look. The outlet dealt in the almost new, the slightly damaged. Geoff clocked the price on a four-chair oak dining room set. From what he could tell, it was an outstanding deal. Ten percent less with the discount. No payments until next year.

Geoff never tired of driving. After the transfer, he drove back to the Kitty Kat for his cut. That afternoon, he pulled into the lot at Treasures. This time he had a reason. Add what he'd scraped together in savings to the cash he'd just pocketed on the crime, he had enough to reclaim his father's knives.

Inside Treasures, he unfolded a wrinkled voucher. An employee with slack, drugged eyes was leaning on the counter. To Geoff's surprise, the employee returned from the vault carrying a cheap plastic beach cooler. Apparently, that's where they'd stored the knives all this time.

"Prepaid," Kitty said, in her bright, minty office. "Three cents per minute domestic and seven overseas. You handle this chore carefully and there may be more boxes falling from trucks, is what I'm saying."

Geoff gently laid his hand on the cardboard box, and Kitty said to him, "Make your parents proud, Geoffrey."

Not long after his felony, Geoff rang Cesar's doorbell. He had an invite for the kid tucked inside a Hallmark, a few Spanish words he'd translated from the book Cesar had left him.

A mocha-faced kid, one of Cesar's roommates, answered the door. He hid behind it. It appeared that, when home, Cesar's roommate liked to dress in a purple nightgown.

"For Cesar," Geoff said, handing him the card. "Make sure he gets this, *comprende?*"

Stupidly, Geoff thought, as he stomped across the lawn toward his open garage, his words had come out loud again.

Geoff packed away coils of coaxial cable, NFL knick-knacks, a stuffed deer's head. He found a good spot for his weight bench in the corner of the garage. In all, he tossed out three extralarge trash bags.

At last, Geoff looked at his new dining room. The four-chair oak dining room set fit nicely under his dusted chandelier.

Scooting kids to proms Geoff could do without, but the money was good.

When the brats lowered the partition, Geoff elevated it. Earlier, before the six boys had hopped in, Geoff had given them the rules, which boiled down to one: do not piss him off. They stood there, six innocent-looking penguins. One boy, the meatiest of the crew, placed an engorged backpack on the leather seat. Geoff ignored the way it clinked.

Some people liked the idea of screwing while traveling around the city. Others sat, blank-faced, devastated after a funeral. Most, however, just sat back and enjoyed the Caddie's status, if only for an hour or two, which was the reason a lot of the faces Geoff came across were young and male.

Fifteen minutes on, Geoff began hearing clapping, followed by howling. Beats from his expensive stereo system rocked the rear cab. He'd once considered attaching a mirror to his front hood. Then he'd be able to see what his passengers were doing out the sunroof.

Geoff pulled off the main boulevard into an older residential area. He figured he'd wait while the kids calmed down.

His phone immediately lit up. A squirrelly voice said, "We said stay on that street."

Geoff set his jaw, thinking briefly about the knives—what he went through to hold on to them.

He slowed. Three maneuvers into a six-point turn, flashes of blue and red filled his side-view mirror.

All these years behind the wheel, Geoff had never, not once, been stopped. The obnoxious music, from behind, faded.

The cop who approached owned a long, bony jaw, and he said to Geoff, "We got a call a limo was leaking beer bottles." The cop said, "One hit a pedestrian."

Geoff didn't have words, so he listened. He thought again about the knives. They were now framed, hanging on his dining room wall.

The cop took Geoff's license. In the darkness, the man appeared to wince. "Sir, your license is expired," the cop said.

Geoff said, "Yeah."

"By six years," the cop said.

Geoff told the man he was sorry, but the cop responded by demanding that Geoff deliver his passengers *now*, make the drop-off early. As in *right now*. Then he informed Geoff of the penalty, a five-hundred-dollar fine, minimum. Plus, he'd also have a nice little face-to-face in front of a judge.

Geoff folded the ticket into his sun visor, tucking it under the faded Kodak of his parents. He hadn't heard a peep come from behind. Geoff drove, and he kept driving until he found a nice little nothing-spot of desert a few miles from anything out in the middle of nowhere. Far off, really far off, a strip mall was lit up like a stadium.

Geoff walked to the trunk and removed a wooden baseball bat he kept for such occasions. He tapped the bat against a tire's rims until the rear door swung open. Then he tapped the rims some more until all six teenagers fumbled out.

The smallest member of the group, a jug-eared kid, said to Geoff, "Shit, you're not my *dad*." He stood gripping the bat. Later, Geoff had to own up to it. The kid's comment stung.

——— ———

That night, Cesar arrived in the same argyle shirt as before. Lines in his hair indicated where he'd carefully combed.

Geoff dragged his old BBQ from the shed and burned the tips on a slab of ribs. He tossed on four ears of corn. He didn't want Cesar going home hungry. He cut lemons into quarters for the iced tea.

Cesar moved gingerly, favoring the side that was healing. The kid was eager to help. Wordlessly, they scooted past each other in Geoff's kitchen, bumping elbows in a way that Geoff found comforting but sad nonetheless.

Geoff set his new dining room table with his great-aunt's china. He served iceberg lettuce salad with great chunks of tomato in it. He refilled Cesar's glass more than once.

When they finally sat down, Cesar bit into a rib, blinked, and said, "*Es delicioso*."

"Yes," Geoff said, "exactly."

All was good this night. His father's knives were home, watching over them from the wall, and when Geoff reached across the table for the butter, the chandelier shot memorable glints of light across the blade of his.

Throughout dinner, Geoff was content watching Cesar eat. A tea droplet dribbled down the kid's chin from his mouth. He was shameless with ugly smiles. And Geoff thought, fingering the fat of a rib, he'd found a place where he could remain still, if it were true.

Holiday
at the
Shamrock

It was July fourth, and they were flushing the jail of misdemeanors and minor infractions, making room for that night's felonies. All morning, Doc was shuffled from pod to hallway, hallway to waiting area, until at last he was handed his street clothes in a brown paper sack and asked by a heavyset deputy to sign out under his own recognizance.

"What's this mean, exactly?" Doc said as he studied the form. Already he'd smudged the words *Failure to Appear* with his thumb.

The deputy licked sweat from his upper lip. "The destruction-of-property charge will be dropped," he said. By signing the document, Doc was promising to clear up the other part, the vagrancy bit, by paying a fine. The previous week, Doc had put a trash can through a pawnshop window. He'd then taken a seat on the curb and waited for the police.

Glass doors parted with a pneumatic pop. Doc stepped into a dry desert oven. It was pushing one hundred five. He waited at a bus stop, sweating acid, and considered the many ways to get rearrested.

The heat punched the brains out of you. You had to look for small comforts to put yourself right. Doc and his fellow cell mates had heard the complaints from staff about the never-ending heat wave. But by day, free to roam the spacious modern pod, and at night, inside their nine-by-nine, temperature-controlled unit, it wasn't a concern.

Freshly hammered tract homes flickered inside the bus windows. The city was strip malls and parking lots nestled inside a brown valley surrounded by mountains. New development spread like ivy, either winding around hills or climbing up them. There was a time Doc lived in one of those pastel boxes, he thought, sucking blood from his gnawed cheek, followed by the time he didn't.

He got off downtown. Work crews were cordoning off streets and erecting blockades. Banners announced the night's big event. Tourists roamed shirtless, and Doc joined the flow. He walked on the lines that cut the street in two, growing aware of an expansive feeling that came with each step.

Tonight, there would be fights. Tonight, there would be drinking. There'd be cursing, kissing and crying, and plenty of scenic mayhem. Tonight, it would be easy to get arrested, if Doc wanted it. Looking his usual, in thinned denim jeans and toeless shoes, he'd just have to hang around and wait for the batons.

He headed to the Shamrock, a place he'd been staying off and on. It was one of dozens of poverty motels that encircled downtown's casino corridor.

Bells chimed on the office door.

"Willie," Doc said to Willie. His friend was slumped at the counter, his finger pegging down a page of *Home and Garden*. The squat Mexican wiped sweat from his forehead.

"I like the look of marble counters," Willie said.

"The heat's boiling you," Doc said.

"Like always," Willie said. "How was vacation?"

"Three meals a day, air-conditioning, and cable television," Doc said. He scooted past the counter toward a storage closet. "The place is packed, is the downside. And they make you wear funny paper shoes."

His backpack was suspended from a broom handle. Inside were dog-eared paperback thrillers and three toothbrushes, still packaged. It was all that Doc owned. He shut the closet.

"Room 312 is yours for eighty this week," Willie said. Beneath hand-painted numerals on the wall were key hooks. Doc noticed 312 in its spot.

"That's up," Doc said. "That's up twenty dollars, in fact."

Willie said, "Holiday prices. Like I told those Salt Lake City kids, it's a holiday."

"Save my room," Doc said.

"Temporary inflation," Willie went on.

"Fine," Doc said.

The previous year, the year Doc walked away and gave up on everything, fireworks sprayed from the bright white roof of the Silver Legacy Casino. The downtown skyline lit up like a sparkler. Sulfur-smelling thunderclaps tore into his lungs, and fleeting bursts of light filled him with such joy that he thought he might collapse. Tonight was going to be a good night, like last year.

The Shamrock, made of red brick, was built in the forties. Doc once leaned against a wall and felt it shift as brick flaked off. He liked the place for its worn-out carpets and sputtering swamp coolers, for its mealy pillows and a lingering stench in the sheets.

Every parking space was stained with motor oil in the sun-cracked lot. Room 217's door was wide open, and Doc called up to it. Blake stepped pantless onto the terrace and swung a pair of jeans around the hot railing, leaning on them.

"Thanks for putting money on the books," Doc called up to him. "I bought candy bars from the commissary. Shared them with my cell mates."

"You'd do the same," Blake said. The kid's Cat in the Hat tattoo glistened on his thick, muscular arm.

Doc said, "What do you say about tonight, outside 312? The fireworks?"

"Sounds good," Blake said.

"If you see Sloppy Bobby, or Barbary, or Connie, tell them too. And ask Willie to come," Doc said. "There's a first-class view from the third-floor landing." Doc added, "And tell your brother."

The brothers were good kids—prizes, if you asked Doc. The three of them shared the same hometown, Salt Lake, and when Doc discovered they also had the Church in common, his questions didn't let up for a week. Who had been their Ward leader? Had they ever been inside the Temple? And wasn't it peculiar, really, how the president considered himself a prophet?

The brothers were running. That much was certain. It was clear by the way Blake's gaze would float off whenever the younger one, Tobias, cracked new light on their former suburban life. Often at the Shamrock, a blurry part of someone's past would briefly come into focus. But it was understood you didn't dig further. Doc knew not to pull up rocks on covered things. If it happened that a person wanted to speak, he spoke. Otherwise, Doc kept his pockets mostly empty and his curiosity clipped when it grew. He knew whom to trust and love and who was kind and who stole kindness from you.

From inside the office, Willie saluted Doc with his rolled-up copy of *Home and Garden*. Regardless of Doc's admonitions about owning a home, about living the responsible life, about phone bills and insurance, dental and vision plans, about drifting ghostlike through bountiful produce sections, he couldn't stop Willie from dreaming about the little homes that punctuated the surrounding hills. There was nothing alive in it for Doc. He'd tried the life. It never fit. That was what the world offered. And he couldn't stop Willie from wanting his thin slice.

Doc found both Frances and T-Bone committing crimes, and he was awed by how vivid everything turned in the late summer glow. To the west, fine white clouds were shot through with orange stripes.

He'd thought about Frances while he was away. He'd thought about the night she stood over him, in bed, after they'd rolled around in room 312. Her eyes sparkled like sequins as she bounced on her toes. The bed vibrated and moaned as he slid nickels into the bedside coin machine. She told Doc she was trying to scratch the ceiling with her fingernails. She was trying to leave her mark.

Frances now cooed over a gray-haired woman parked on a bench. The woman was cradling her purse. She held it like a mother does a child.

"I love you, baby," Frances was saying. She walked her fingers across a liver spot on the old woman's forearm. "Come on, baby darling, let me see what's inside."

Frances never looked properly dressed. She was famous for rummaging vibrant pieces of fabric from mall dumpsters and then wrapping her small body in them. Doc couldn't place the exact country, an Asian one. Frances looked exactly like those poles with their billowing flags.

"I love you, doll, can't you see?" Frances said. The old woman's eyes remained lowered. Frances said to Doc, "I'm telling this nice lady we should be friends."

"You're doing fine," Doc said. "But look, it's the Fourth. Remember?"

Frances said, "Oh."

Doc invited her to the gathering, but she'd only accept on one condition—that Doc help with her predicament. So, together, they gently peeled the woman's bony pink fingers and pried open her storm-shutter arms. Frances dipped her hand inside the woman's purse and came out with a bloated wallet.

The way they designed casino floors, they wanted you to feel adrift and disoriented by the noise and the lights and the mirrors, and it pretty much worked. It was easy to lose money when the money lost was lost inside of a dream.

Doc preferred the Sands. The Sands was pleasant. It had a pool where he sometimes cleaned up. Years ago, he'd stayed in a suite during a chiropractors' conference. Now the Sands had gone the way of the bigger places. They used a plastic-card slot system instead of coins.

So Doc hiked to the Purple Coyote instead.

He wandered the aisles until he placed his mark. An overweight woman in a lime-colored dress was playing two machines at once. She played passionately, athletically, as though the deeper she sank her hopes into those chrome mouths, the more buoyant her jackpot became. One good sign was the number of scattered beer bottles between her machines. Even better, several coin trays were hiding among the empties.

Doc loitered on the opposite aisle. He watched the woman hop in place. It was as though he were at the library, stalking a stranger on the other side of the stacks. By its weight, Doc estimated, as he strolled confidently toward the exit, the woman's tray held enough for a room and a very fine night.

Outside, Doc was startled by the sight of his friend T-Bone leaning against a parking meter. T-Bone's arm was in a cast, had been for some time. But the bandage around his other wrist was new.

"What's with your wrist?" Doc asked.

T-Bone was thirty, maybe forty years old. They knocked knuckles.

"Some big hero type came out of his building and broke my arm," T-Bone said. "And last week, when you were on vacation, that same hero came out of the same building and twisted my wrist to shit. Just because I fiddled with his meter."

"Little room for mercy in this world," Doc said.

T-Bone rotated a piece of bent metal inside the lock. "A man's got to make do, I told him," T-Bone went on. The meter clicked. Its face swung open.

"How much you got?" Doc asked.

"About fifty in change," T-Bone said. He made a pouch with his T-shirt. Coins cascaded into it. "More now."

Doc said, "Want to double up on a room?"

When T-Bone smiled, he had small teeth, squared corn kernels. "Sure enough," he said.

Doc didn't know where T-Bone disappeared winters. Summers, he usually camped riverside, on the grounds of a condominium development. He invited Doc once. Doc saw how T-Bone had cut a hole in a chain-link fence, how T-Bone had fastened a bike rim around the opening, lending his entrance that same chain-link appearance while simultaneously making a doorway.

After a twenty-three–quarter meal, deducted from his seventy-dollar take, Doc sat on a ledge planted with yellow dahlias. A sting pierced his cracked lips whenever he smiled at the people milling in the closed-off streets. Their expressions were feisty, full of life, and Doc didn't really mind the mothers who guided their teen-agers away, or the guilty stares from the older folks, or even the drunken slurs that came from men with strange tans. The streets were burning, swarmed, and alive.

A Jack Daniels bottle sailed through the air, spinning clockwise, and soon it was lost as it fell into a grouping of rodeo men singing loudly in the gathering crowd. Evening came.

Doors at the Shamrock opened, and people walked freely along the open-air landings. Smiles were heatstroked but happy, and three men Doc knew as alcoholics huddled by the ice machine, sucking relief from cubes.

Frances was there. T-Bone too. Blake and his brother, Tobias, waited outside room 312 with unopened bottles clinking inside a cardboard box. Sloppy Bobby was there, and Barbary, and Willie handed him a key. Even the sad mother from 208, whose thirteen-year-old had run away, she was there with them to watch the dizzying light show that concussed their hearts and numbed their gums.

They drank from clear plastic cups and witnessed the sky tremble. Aerials pulsed upward and flowered into chrysanthemums. The brothers passed bottles. Doc laughed along with people on the sidewalk. Puny firecrackers popped up and down alleyways while massive bursts fell like glittering rain. Orbs of fast-moving light ripped into smoke drifts. Doc held his breath that final moment before it was over, when a galaxy of stars pushed down.

One fading star landed across the street on top of the Ante-Up. T-Bone shook his bandaged wrist, pointing. The long hot summer must have dried out the roof, because it went up fast. Doc soon felt heat behind his eyes. On the street below, the crowd swayed, uncertain of its direction.

Closed doors quickly swung open. Doc and the others lined the balconies, watching the Ante-Up's residents gather the little they owned. One elderly man, his wet eyes marking another defeat, descended a stairwell with a terra-cotta pot. Purple orchids dangled from a spike.

Fire engines slowly maneuvered through the mass of people. Everyone forgot about the fireworks, mesmerized instead by the strange hallucination of red tails writhing throughout the Ante-Up.

Doc picked ash from Frances's hair.

"What's your wish?" he asked. And she held his hand against her warm neck.

Flames unfurled from windows, licking the air. Dazed faces marched across the street, through the crowd, toward their neighbors at the Shamrock.

Some regulars, Doc knew, would take from these strangers. Some residents at the Shamrock ate glass while stealing a person's shoes. Then there was everyone else. Frances, Willie, T-Bone, Blake, and Tobias—friends who ached for gifts like this night.

There was room at the Shamrock. There was room, and they welcomed them.

The
Bulls at
San Luis

The price tag on the Night Owl Infrared Specs was steep, but the binoculars do the job. Amplify starlight. Invert darkness. Organize the desert into Cye's X-ray.

A green-tinted figure roams into Cye's lens. "*Uno.*" He sees another. He starts the math. "Two."

This is Cye's second run in a month. He's nicknamed the rendezvous El Cementerio because several large, wind-chiseled boulders have eroded in the shape of headstones. Rumor has it, beneath every other rock near the border is a grave. Out here, along the line, Cye believes it.

He counts nine men a half mile away. They're kicking up a hell of a dust cloud, and they're late but on target. Cye flips a lever under his dash. A strobe attached to his front grill begins to pulse. His Suburban becomes a beacon. When the group spots him, they turn.

In the three years he's been running illegals, Cye's seen his share. When he's not playing hide-and-seek with Bronco-patrolling border cops, he's watching missile-heavy jets lay fume trails across the sky. Even when his passengers avoid the bombs, the sunlight inflicts its varying punishments. Heat exhaustion, dehydration, hyperthermia, or some combination-of.

Night is the time to hustle. At night, when darkness cools the badlands, the border stirs.

El Cementerio is outside *la migra's* reach. Cye picked the place because it rests inside the Barry M. Goldwater Air Force Range, a great chunk of hot Arizona desert that cuddles the Mexico line. Kicker is, illegals must haul ass twenty miles or so across an active bombing range to make it.

Before the big walk, they're lined up and pep-talked.

"Eviten los tanques." The U.S. Army retires tanks out there. And the Air Force bombs those tanks, *entienden?*

Some people don't listen, of course. Folks climb into abandoned Bradleys to find shade, *tener sexo*, whatever. A bunker buster once honed in on some poor *pendejo* as he was pinching a loaf inside a WWII Sherman. Cye was later given the replay: the blast turned the guy's ass into a crater.

Immigrant trails demand sacrifice. Cye understands this, but lately the stories have begun to eat at him. Every sad report forces introspection, which he hates. Worst-case scenario, he could always take matters into his own. If the time comes, when the time comes, he could always wander into the scorched flats, walk until he couldn't anymore, and sit beside a rock with his name on it. Sure, something like that.

Hints of creosote waft through the window and settle on Cye's tongue. He flips on a light, and the side-view mirror captures his profile. The sun has deepened lines beside both eyes. He's also going prematurely gray. White wires jut from his temples.

It's been almost a year since the asshole in Phoenix handed Cye a leaflet, "Preparing for Your Illness." Cye shredded it. For days afterward, he wondered if the physician predicted that kind of response. Bloating, an occasional lightning rod of pain, Cye tries not to acknowledge his terminal disease. He tries not to lend it authority over his remaining time.

From out of the darkness, the illegals emerge, one by one. Aglow in his headlights, the nine men look exhausted. Arms hang heavily from shoulders. *El desierto* has left them speechless.

Often, Cye wonders what his passengers think of his blue eyes, a trait inherited from his *gringo* dad. He wonders if the color elicits quiet judgments. Cye's always thought the rest of him—his dark complexion, his thick hair, and sloping cheekbones—belong to his *madre*, to *Sinaloa*, to *México*.

La migra have their job: tracking, spotting, chasing. And Cye's got his.

In the dry Arizona lowlands, Cye plays Moses. On drop-offs, when he nails the destination, dudes wrap him in hugs. *Señoritas* pinch his ass. Old women drape rosaries around his neck.

"*Mi mejor conductor*," El Jefe likes to say about Cye. "*Un fabricante del dinero*." His best driver, a real moneymaker.

Border crossing is an act of faith. Cye believes in the principle. He believes in salvation and exodus, that big march into the Promised Land. Most places, the border's nothing more than a useless strand of barbed wire, a total joke.

Cye's boss, El Jefe, the people broker, runs operations out of Ciudad Juárez, just over the bridge from El Paso. Cye met Jefe in Phoenix years ago, in English 1A, day one of community college. Back then, Jefe was a bucktoothed *cholo* wannabe, and Cye was rearranging his late twenties, drying out, deluding himself into believing he wanted to repair air conditioners. The first day of class, Jefe sat next to Cye, accidentally bumped his foot, and confessed that he was there to polish the more important verbs: buy, sell, own.

Inside Jefe's cramped cinderblock office, he's now got satellite phones and a Rolodex full of business. Excel spreadsheets radiate from laptops. Stacks of new Blackberries are piled in the corner, waiting to be used, each gadget registered to a nonexistent person. El Jefe arranges the loads. He faxes Cye quantities, times, and dates.

"*Pinche gringos* need us," El Jefe likes to say. Jefe has a crazy set of long teeth that overlap a fat bottom lip.

Dry erase boards sit propped on easels. Jefe draws contour maps on them, marking flow points. He likes embellishing his sketches of desert peaks, turning burnt mountain ranges into columns of too-perfect breasts. Jefe also has the habit of signing the dry erase boards with looping Js which look like snakes, as though the synchronized machinery of his operation is a work of art.

When certain corridors of the border become overcrowded, Jefe simply erases the paths and repositions them. The paths always lead north.

"Two thousand miles of invisible highway," El Jefe also likes to say, his teeth clomping down on his lip. "And the flow is strong, cabrón. The flow is relentless."

Stopping it, Cye knows, is like stopping a tsunami with a tennis racket. During election years, sure, the Feds always put on a show. They hoist stadium lights, concoct new strategies, rally Congress for more funds, for more symbolic fenceline. Traffic only gets redirected, to the most desolate regions, to rural hick-spots, to the desert.

Cye memorizes old dirt roads and alternate short cuts. He counts the faces. He moves the people. Totaling up his cut, he has one-hundred-eighty grand saved. The money's stuffed inside hollowed-out aerosol cans, a pantry's worth, in his rarely used apartment in Mesa.

Cye's a simple man. He likes his apartments spotless, unfurnished, and easy to maintain. He considered buying a house once, in Vegas, on the links. He even squirreled away a down payment, more than enough. But after the diagnosis, he reneged at the last minute, disappointing the attractive real estate broker and, not surprisingly, any shot at a date.

Cye pops the locks. The men pile in, wrestling for room. They argue with their elbows. Mostly, the damage is to their cheeks, arms, and necks, which are burned, tender. Cye distributes water bottles. Five of the men are dressed in blue tracksuits, like a team. Except for a fine coating of dust, the suits look new, as though the quintet saved up for their Arizona debut.

Cye says, "If you're near one, a seat belt, use it."

The youngest, a teenager, decides to take the front passenger seat. The kid's upper lip is latticed with cracks and his eyes nictitate, a trace of buzz melting from them. Cye knows he's been chewing MetaboThin diet pills, a favorite among border jumpers. Ephedrine helps pick up the clip on the long walk.

Cye tosses a gallon jug in the kid's lap, nailing him matter-of-factly. "Seat belt, *por favor*," he says.

The kid's wounded gaze drifts to Cye's earlobe, pausing on his turquoise stud.

Cye stays quiet during the drive. He likes fiddling with the stereo, listening to AM sports talk. Mostly, he eavesdrops. He enjoys the men's stories. Cye's mom is *mestiza*. She crossed under the radar in the sixties. Growing up, she nagged his dad in English but rattled off Spanish when talking to her son. So when there's talk, he understands.

It's a short, bouncy ride to I-8. Cye hits pavement, leaving the dirt road behind. He races toward northbound 95, which will shuttle them to Nevada.

Discussion arises among the five men in tracksuits. Three of them are stacked like tuna cans in the rear cargo area. Turns out they're brothers, from Oaxaca. Manny, the ringleader, does all the talking. Apparently the brothers worked for a time at a *maquiladora* in Nogales. They had fifty-cent-an-hour, ten-hours-a-day shit jobs, folding cardboard boxes, then packing tennis shoes into them. The pay sucked, workers were mistreated, etc.

Manny made the call. They hadn't tried *los Estados Unidos*. Yeah, he says, decorating his sentences with his hands, he figured they should try Vegas. When Manny says Vegas, he means it. He forms a fist and punches one hand with the other: *Vegas*.

El Jefe advanced the brothers the fare: sixteen thousand pesos per person.

So yeah, Manny says, the deal is they'll crash at one of Jefe's houses. They'll work and repay the loan—meaning, Cye knows, plus ten interest points.

Cye counts shrines along northbound 95. Periodically his high beams light up a new roadside memorial. By his estimate, he's spotted thirteen, one more than on his previous run. Cye floats scenarios at each sighting: a blowout, resulting in loss of control.

Or some drunken old fart, asleep at the wheel, wrapping it around a guardrail.

South of Parker, Arizona, Cye trolls the roadside, looking for number fourteen. His passengers are completely wiped out. Every hard shoulder has become a pillow. The journey for them is twelve hours under hot sun plus seven more on the road.

Thinking he missed it, Cye considers doubling back. At last, he pulls up alongside a rickety white cross. Propped against the cross is a cheap drugstore wreath, its plastic petals shriveled into kernels.

He began caretaking not long after his diagnosis. He found the spot by accident during a midnight shuttle ride. A piss break, dropped trou, cold air nipping his crack. He was aiming his stream at a large saguaro when he realized he was standing on a dirt-covered cross. Duct-taped to it was a smudged Kodak snapshot of a young couple, decked out in tuxedo and wedding dress. The young white man in the picture sported an Oakland Raiders cap. Next to him stood a pretty Latina, her forehead covered with pimples.

Cye was struck. This was where the couple died. The thought electrified him in shivers. He ran a finger over the girl's face, over her pimply brow, imagining he could feel the bumps, that he could read her like Braille.

That night, he began to dig. A hole opened, and he resurrected the cross and reinforced it with rocks. He gave them names: Richard and Eva, after his parents, another mixed pair.

For so many years Cye never paid attention—this, that, whatever. He was always consumed by bars and the women in them, followed later by gas stations and cash drops and *hola, adiós*. Nowadays, Cye's been growing more aware of tributes in all their forms. Streets, names of towns, rivers. Denver is named in honor of James Denver, and so on.

Cye grabs a plastic grocery bag from under his seat. It's filled with candles, little white numbers he bought at the Dollar Depot in Tempe. The candles are small, with white wax, encased in clear glass.

Chilled nighttime air opens his sinuses. Affixed to the cross's left arm with fishing wire is a new Raiders ball cap. Cye left it his last visit. He's an Arizona Cardinals fan. He despises the Raiders. But the gesture felt important.

The couple's memorial isn't the great pyramid, but it's something. In a year, maybe less, it'll be gone, who knows. And it's impossible not to wonder. How was their last second? Terrifying? How much blood and pain?

Cye lights two candles, one for her, one for him. He shields them with rocks, protecting the flames from a breeze. Stapled to the couple's photo is a note. Blue paper, folded, and until now Cye hasn't dared to touch it. He figures it's probably some pathetic poem, some sister's hysterical letter. On the one hand, learning about Richard and Eva could ruin them for him. That's the deal with getting to know people. Then there's the other hand. The note could teach him something. Maybe tell him how not to worry. Maybe give him guidance.

Cye doesn't sit well with indecision. He removes the staple and shoves the note in his pocket.

When he opens the driver-side door, the kid's eyes slam shut. He's pretending to be asleep. The kid has been watching, which makes Cye feel responsible. A shiny glaze of saliva rings the kid's mouth. Over the past few hours, Cye's monitored the boy's dirty little habit.

Cye says to him, "You're making love to that thumb. Maybe your mouth should find a better target."

Long drives exacerbate Cye's symptoms—nausea, no appetite, heartburn, etc. It's as though an animal is hibernating in his gut, distending his intestines.

Cye shuts down the air. Without it, the cabin fills with the cruel stink of men and sweat. The sun crowns between two mountains and floods the cabin with light. Soon the murmuring begins. Distances close between highway Mini Mart sightings. The men know they are drawing close. Already it's pushing ninety degrees.

In the daytime, Vegas shines. All that sun, all those hotel windows. *El Norte*, especially Vegas, means payday. Vegas is industry. Expansion demands cheap, capable hands needed for landscaping, laundry, and drywall. Twice a month, Cye makes a drop, and the drop pays well. El Jefe's got contracts with several outfits.

In an industrial district near the airport, Cye pulls into a lot encircled by chain-link. The lot sits under an overpass. Above, bikini-clad breasts painted on a billboard publicize a strip-club chain. At night Cye's seen them; neon nipples shaped like arrows point at the off-ramp.

Hernan is waiting, as usual, leaning against a teal-colored Chevy. He's El Jefe's go-to in Vegas. Cye's never been bothered by Hernan. He's a business type, an aficionado of silk shirts, gold chains, and pilot glasses that shield two bulging eyes.

"That billboard makes me want to play grab ass," Cye says to Hernan, stepping down from his rig.

Hernan holds a clipboard. As each man climbs out, Hernan ticks a box on a form.

"The Grand Admiral," Hernan says. He never stops talking business. "You know, that new three-billion-dollar casino? They're excavating a lake. Preparing for yachts. Races. We need hands," he goes on.

Cye says, "Yachts?"

"For the marina," Hernan says.

Cye says, "Marina?"

The young kid walks over with his hand extended. His smile opens a thin wound on his damaged lip. When Cye takes the kid's grip, it feels as though a sword enters through his belly button. It twists.

Cye doubles over, desperate for a breath. It's difficult to swallow. And the afterpain is warm, sharp, like he's been brass-knuckled. The first time this happened, he thought of coyote traps snapping around his midsection. That pain was particularly toothy.

"*Qué te pasa?*" Hernan says.

Cye says, "Too much driving, man." He pinches a roll of love-handle fat. "Gas, I think. I don't know. Haven't eaten." He's pre-rehearsed his lies.

As he crouches (crouching curbs the throbs), he scrutinizes the men he delivered, measuring their anxious shifts. For a moment, he's frightened by a vision of their skin peeling away, unfurling like old wallpaper, and their skeletons peeking through.

That horrible afternoon in Phoenix—in fact, the worst afternoon of Cye's fucking life—he nearly tossed up the chalky barium concoction in the doctor's face. Six, the specialist said—what, seven months? Cye's standing on month eight, without treatment, so what's the guy know? *Está loco,* Cye thinks. He refuses to buy in to some countdown.

"Listen," Hernan says. He distributes paperwork to the illegals, fake work documents. "We got this *puñeta* over there," Hernan says. He directs Cye toward the gate with his pen. "Guy told me, in so many words, he wants to be dropped. He wants to go back."

Cye looks over. A middle-aged man is standing next to a suitcase. He's *mestizo*: squat, black hair, the standard. But this guy is dressed in a brown suit, as though he's ready for something special. Indeed.

"Back?" Cye says to Hernan.

"Over the line," Hernan says.

Cye says, "Who goes back?"

The stranger also wears a cinnamon-colored Stetson. A crisp white button-up accentuates his dark skin.

"So, where's your guitar?" Cye says to the stranger when he walks over.

The man says, "*Qué?*"

"You miss the traveling ranchero bus or something?"

The man draws down his eyelids, indicating his annoyance. "I need to get to Interstate 8," the man says. Traces of Mexican shrapnel scar his English. "There's a rest area outside Yuma," he goes on.

Another thing, the man's left front tooth is gold-capped. There's a cutout in the center. A tiny white heart in the middle flashes when the man speaks. Distracting.

Cye says, "This ride is usually one-way."

"You live in Arizona, I hear," the man says. "Hernan tells me you're driving back this afternoon."

Cye breathes deeply. His airways open. The pain is fading. He's seen this sort of thing before. He knows the man can't just skate over like everyone else because he lacks paperwork. Without paperwork, he could be hassled or arrested. Without papers you're as good as invisible, as though papers prove a beating heart. Typical bullshit. Life limited by government formalities and imaginary lines.

Cye says, "*La Migra* set up checkpoints around there. That area spoons the border. So you know," he says, "what I'm saying is, I'd be taking a risk dropping you."

From his suit pocket, the man pulls out a wad of green. He peels off five bills.

Lately, Cye's been searching for excuses, reasons to give it up, remain in bed, say to hell with everything. Somehow he finds the muscles required to scrape a toothbrush across his gums. One foot in front of the other, in front of the other.

Midafternoon, the drive south is two walls of brown and straight, white highway lines. Cye's passenger, turns out, is named Nunez, but that's about as much info as Cye's able to extract after fifty-something miles. Nunez, apparently, enjoys the quiet. But quiet makes road trips unpleasant. Quiet tends to hum like a busted refrigerator. Cye's usually got a cab full of yammering illegals. Arguments, debates. Cye doesn't trust the quiet. Silence has a way of turning his thoughts into bombs.

Cye shoves in a cassette tape, tinkering with the volume. He says, "I've seen a few accidents on this stretch of road."

Nunez ignores the bait. He chooses to stare out the window, as though he's communing with the landscape, its monotonous browns and crimsons. Those hands of his are restless, though. Nunez twirls a gold band around his marriage finger. At least the guy shrugged off his suit jacket. Thing was making Cye sweat.

Cye says, "Six months ago, this guy in front of me, driving a Jeep, his heart exploded. I watched the crash through the windshield like a movie." He says, "Dude swerved to the right, hit the shoulder, overcompensated the wheel, and took out a Pontiac in the oncoming lane."

This is high-quality material, topical. Everyone enjoys firsthand tragedy stories. But not Nunez. Nunez continues his ridiculousness, saying nothing. A distant look clouds his eyes as he fingers his goddamn ring. Cye moves up Nunez's wrists, noticing a pair of cuff links ornamented with miniature black bulls. Not only that, an elaborate, embroidered *N* adorns his shirt pocket.

Cye wonders what the big production is all about, especially the gold tooth with the heart. What business does Nunez have traipsing through the desert looking like Ramon Novarro? Nunez wants to be taxied into bomb country, near El Cementerio, right inside *migra* cutting lanes and migrant footpaths. Sure, Nunez could nosedive south and walk twelve desperate hours. If he hustled, he could make it. In fact, he'd likely pass crews moving north.

Cye says, after a while, "Be nice if there was somewhere to go with my words." He says, "Be nice if you spoke."

Nunez pinches his chin, and he says, "Road signs look venomous." At last, a sentence. It's like pulling molars. "Blacks and yellows, the striped kind," Nunez says. "Reminds me of snakes and spiders. Maybe they do that to help people avoid accidents. Scare them. So people pay attention to the road."

Cye shoots Nunez a hard sideways glance. He imagines pulling over, smashing that little gold trinket out of Nunez's grin. Instead, he pops the cassette tape out, scanning the AM dial. The only station with reasonable reception is public radio, the BBC. Cye listens resentfully: soccer scores of European teams he doesn't know, delivered via some effete-sounding dickhead. Cye's never traveled outside the lower forty-eight.

A pathetic stream parallels the highway, dipping under sage, appearing again. Eventually the land drinks it away. On these long round-trips, Cye stops midway, in Quartzsite, a former mining town. A highway sign points out that Quartzsite is twenty miles up-road. Cye's never liked the place, with its gas stations, countless mobile homes, and nothing to do, but dried sweat granules are caked on his back. And his palms and knuckles ache. A hot shower, he thinks, sleep.

Before they pull off, Cye gestures to Nunez's ring, and he says, "All right, you got me. Who's behind the hot property?"

Nunez shows that little heart of his, wet with saliva.

"Eloisa," Nunez says. He says the ring connects him to her, his children, everyone important in Mexico. He says, "People never ask."

Cye drives to the Arroyo. The motel is on a dead-end street, rimmed on either side by crumbling, pink adobe walls. It's an unremarkable building. A frayed Mexican flag billows from a rust-covered pole. Cye uses the motel for overnights, midrun logistics, and so on. Over the past six months, he's clocked more than twenty thou on his odometer. At the Arroyo, the beds are free.

As usual, Fausto's in the office watching TV, couch-lounging, his hand buried inside a box of kid's cereal.

Cye says, stepping inside, "Dingdong."

"Oh," Fausto says, looking up. "Jefe mentioned something about you."

At six-foot-five, Fausto's the tallest Mexican that Cye's ever met. Fausto was once a star JC ballplayer in Phoenix. But he tore his ACL before graduating to Division I. His wide skull makes his face look stretched, his cheekbones polished.

Cye says, "Caught a sliver of the Bruins game on the radio."

"I don't want to hear it," Fausto says. His exhale signals disappointment. He picks through a pile of green, saguaro-shaped key chains inside an old coffee can. He says, "Poor season for State."

"That UCLA point guard shot the lights out," Cye says.

Fausto changes direction. "Anyway, look at you. Start hitting the weight bench or something?" He says, "You're getting lean."

It's hard for Cye to admit, but he has shed body weight, poundage. Cye says, "Funny." He changes direction, too. "We have a guest, so I need another key."

The Arroyo's No Vacancy sign is always lit. El Jefe owns the place. It's a shelter company he uses to launder money, store illegals, etc. Fausto's only responsibility is to report a full house nightly. This way, a portion of Jefe's dirty bills hop onto the books, cleaned.

Cye settles into room 18. Before he can get comfortable, Nunez raps loudly on his window. Nunez tells him some funny news about a two-foot-long Gila Monster inside his bathroom. Cye follows Nunez, and sure enough, the thing is hiding behind the toilet, its skinny forked tongue darting in and out. Lumps of gray shit are caked to the tiles.

Cye finds Fausto in the office. "Can Nunez get a room without reptiles, please?" he says.

Cye slashes his drapes shut. Prior to stepping into the shower, he washes a large brown spider down the drain. Steam blooms, warming the cold bathroom, and for a moment Cye stands completely still, liberated from his jeans and socks. Naked suits him.

He tries to avoid the thought, but he can't escape it. He will miss the feeling.

And has he been working out, asks Fausto. That smart-ass. Still, Cye has begun cinching his belt tighter. His jeans hang looser.

About Cye's rotting stomach, El Jefe knows nothing. Neither does his mom or dad. Fact is, Cye hasn't shared the test results with anyone. When worries about his condition arise, fear nukes them into oblivion. He focuses instead on errands, sports, anything, whatever.

Nothing can be done, however, about constant reminders. Lately, deep red blood-strings streak his morning toilet bowl.

Later, Cye stares at a spiderweb clinging for its life. It sways in the corner from the fan's airstream. A knock comes at the door. He shuffles over, towel around his waist.

"Look what I found," Nunez says. He lifts two sixers of Tecate, cans. "I also found two folding chairs behind that dumpster," he says.

Cye peers outside. Nunez has assembled a little outdoor lounge, complete with buckets of ice from the machine. Cye wonders how Nunez suddenly found nice. His Stetson is gone, same with his jacket and dress shirt. He's whittled himself down to a white T-shirt and shorts.

"Fifteen minutes of remaining daylight," Nunez says. "So I thought, why not?"

Cye jumps into jeans. Gusts of warm air tangle his hair, breeze-drying it. Nunez hands him a can, and Cye says, popping the beer, "You never said. People usually can't stop talking about their experience. Blah blah. Biggest decision of their lives. The border cross."

Nunez pours rim foam onto the cement. "I'm following the money I made home," he says. "That's all."

Cye nods. "Makes sense."

"I worked. I sent back what I earned," Nunez says. "And I learned to forget that night we came over. I'm right here, next to you. But I am always in Veracruz."

"Sounds a bit like living in the middle."

"For six years," Nunez says.

The beer tastes like aluminum, liquid nickels, how Cye likes it. A television drones in the office. Except for Fausto, who's busy flipping through TV channels, the motel is empty. Poor Fausto. First that knee of his, and now he's serving time at the Arroyo. El Jefe got word Fausto was dealing exotic reptiles at swap meets, earning side cash. Selling lizards isn't a big deal, but it is a crime. And extracurricular pursuits that could bring sideways heat on Jefe is a no-no. Rule number one, *cabrón*.

Quartzsite isn't much of a town, and there isn't much ambient light. Soon Nunez's face disappears under a curtain of shadows. The outdoor bulbs don't light up. Cye notices that there aren't any bulbs, just a row of empty sockets. Damn Fausto.

Cye returns from the Suburban with three candles.

"We're full of surprises tonight," Nunez says.

The soft, flickering glow dyes the red Tecate cans, making them appear warm, like coals. Cye was up all night, and his stomach registers it. All this back-and-forth is exhausting. The demand never stops. He hasn't had a full night for what feels like weeks, so when he pops another beer, he considers it a sleep aid.

"You know, we're not far from a crossing station," Cye says. He tumbles into his chair. The beer has already made his eardrums buzz. He says, "There's a small border shack a few hours south. I could drive you there. Sure as hell beats the desert."

Nunez shakes his head. "I want to walk it."

"People die on that walk," Cye says. He wants Nunez to understand. "I mean, it happens. It's a full day of walking through nowhere."

"I've heard," Nunez says.

So. Nunez owns that particular brand of confidence. Just like Cye's mom, foolish and proud. It makes Cye feel reduced.

He holds his beer can over a candle. He considers extinguishing it. A strand of heat rises from its rolling flame. Cye warms his fingernail on the flame instead, watching how a delicate, invisible heat stream displaces the air around it. He's unable to distinguish, near its hot tip, where the flame tapers and where the air begins. It is flame, and then, simply, it is nothing, a disappearance.

"Still," Cye says, considering Nunez's wish, "that hike is a hell of a thing."

"*Deseo ir a mi país,*" Nunez says. He wants to go home. Cye senses the weight of Nunez's eyes. He dislikes the feeling of someone trying to read him.

"Foolish," Cye says. This man has a choice. And that choice is reckless. Ending the conversation, Cye says, "Goddamn stubborn."

When the evening turns chilly, Nunez excuses himself, leaving Cye alone. Cye stacks his empties—three, five, seven. Every so often, he lowers a finger into the dying flame. After tempting it one too many times, he manages to singe himself, curling a few small hairs. He burns his skin too, just when he thought, stupidly, he was beginning to master the distance.

In the morning, Cye wakes early. He tosses in bed, bargaining with his pillow. He pinches it between his kneecaps. Sheets spool around his legs. He'll give everything back, his money, his Suburban, especially all his crap decisions. He will do better. During early morning hours he can sense the end rushing toward him. It feels like cold fingers pinching his throat, a slight shift in his chest cavity.

Cye stares at the note he stole off the highway cross. It sits on the end table. After a one-rinse shower, he pockets it.

Cye pounds on Nunez's door, and when Nunez answers, his eyelids are struggling. It's before dawn. They should head out, grab a bite, Cye says, bouncing on his heels. "I should drop you before the sun turns radioactive."

Daytime crosses are easier, Cye explains to Nunez as they drive south. He taps the wheel with both thumbs. "*Migra* aren't out en masse, like at night." But daytime crosses are dangerous, when the sun's highest, hottest, when the flats are stunning but at their absolute worst. Cye recites the horrors he's seen: grown men crying, tottering on their heels, as though they'd daytripped through hell. Delirious eyes staring out from behind cracked, Gucci-imitation sunglasses. And then their minds, fully sun-drugged, their discombobulated words hitting the air diagonally.

"Not too late to just drive over," Cye says. He awaits a response from Nunez, but it doesn't come.

A diamondback basks in the middle of Interstate 8, west out of Yuma. Cye pit-stops at a pancake joint and orders six-deep flapjacks. He smothers the load in syrup. Nunez picks blueberries off the lid of a muffin. Lukewarm coffee slices through Cye's seven-beer hangover, while a bonfire builds in the pit of his stomach. He envisions a scalpel peeling off stomach lining. The fuckhead in Phoenix instructed Cye to eliminate alcohol, coffee, sugar—shit, everything he likes.

"Truly a man of few words," Cye says to Nunez, who's sitting quietly opposite. Nunez offers a small smile. Like the day before, he's dressed to the nines. They hop into the Suburban and drive on.

Desert is the perfect liar. Distances deceive. Everything appears closer than. You have to respect and understand the land, or else.

Nunez tips the visor, denying a rising sun. Again, his attention wanders off into the view. He follows the landscape's rigid lines, its shadows produced by cliffs. Mesquite trees bathe in an endless amber sea.

Nunez says, quite suddenly, "I crossed with my friend Enrique." His Stetson bounces on his knee. "We came over at San Luis. That area was just abandoned ranches. And big sand lots."

Cye wants to draw him out, open him up. He says, "Right. Still lots of both."

"There was a larger ranch," Nunez says. "Mexican owned. It bled over the line."

"That so?" Cye says. Every border brother has a story. "You came over at night?"

Nunez nods. "We were a group. The guide we paid drove us to a field. He told us, crawl. And when we see horns, he said, go low, and crawl. That land was shredded. Bulls roamed it. Thousand-pound Brahmans with those long *burro* ears. Ever seen those?"

Cye says, "I don't believe so."

"The guide told us that *la migra* didn't patrol private land. Enrique counted for hours. One hundred bulls. Two hundred. We crept around them. It was what we had to do. Through dried-up piss clods and *mierda*. When some of the others stood to walk, *los toros* panicked. Two boys were trampled." Nunez traces the brim of his Stetson. "But Enrique and I crawled," he says. "And we moved low, in shit, and the beasts didn't mind us."

A quick, uncomfortable sadness overcomes Cye. He imagines a dark field sprinkled with easily spooked bulls and desperate men.

In the northbound lane, they both spot a checkpoint, two *migra* Broncos and a long white passenger van.

"See what I said," Cye says.

A row of heads, obviously illegals, decorates the van's windows like stilled *muñecas*.

Cye says, "They'll be fingerprinted, escorted back. Same old."

"Until next try," Nunez says.

"Right," Cye says.

Cye decides to dirt-road it. An inlet in the brush leads them south. At a crossroads, where Cye usually turns for El Cementerio, he drives straight. After a few miles, he knows he can stop at any time, drop Nunez, earn the five bills. But he keeps going. He wants to give Nunez a better-than-usual shot.

Cye knows of a dry floodwash. They drop downslope into it, tearing along the dusty playa. Soon they enter the Barry Goldwater Range, marked with yellow government signs, their stern military warnings long since defaced.

Nunez says, "Anywhere is good. Anywhere."

Cye doesn't stop. They pass a gigantic B-52 warplane embedded sideways into the earth. One wing points skyward and throws a long westward shadow, like a sundial. Across its side are gaping holes. Clearly it's been shelled. When the floodplain vanishes, Cye drives into a rocky open bowl. Brush scrapes his chassis.

It's the closest Cye's been to the border. There's no evidence of any line or boundary whatsoever. It's just rocks and cacti. In the distance, the bald peaks of the Tinajas Atlas Mountains smolder. Heat has already begun seeping through the windows. The air-conditioning can't contain it.

"Okay," Cye says, stopping. He stares ahead, gripping the wheel. "Okay," he says again.

A small bird pops from a pared hole in a nearby saguaro. Cye asks himself how that thing survives with all this constant pressure.

Nunez stuffs water bottles into his suitcase, adding more weight.

"Sure that outfit is the smartest idea?" Cye says to him. Even imagining walking through this baked desert in a suit makes him feel miserable.

Nunez dons his Stetson, crowning it all off. It's that toothy heart again, twinkling inside Nunez's mouth. And he says, "Think of the bulls." He says, "That night, and the men and the bulls. I crawled over in shit, *compadre*. I owe it to myself to walk back. My own two feet." Nunez struggles with the suitcase, counterbalancing to his left. Without a handshake, not even *adiós*, he turns and walks away.

He'll make it, Cye thinks. Nunez is like Cye's mom. He's that type. He has to make it.

Querida Rosa, reads the first line. Behind the wheel, Cye unfolds the crumpled note. It's a short paragraph, chicken-scratched in red ink. Turns out, it's a letter from the dead girl's mother. So. The girl's name is Rosa. Nineteen-year-old Rosa. *Querida Rosa . . .*

Third line in, Rosa's mother misspells the word *children*. *Childen*. She forgot her goddamn *r*. The mistake bothers Cye. How careless. Again he reads the lines, seven in all, which skip between English and Spanish, and he waits for the mother's sad, angry words to hook him in the throat and crush his lungs.

But nothing happens. Nothing happens, he realizes, because these words don't belong to him. They belong to a girl once named Rosa, a teenager who haunts the side of a lonely highway, who now lives inside others and on this lost piece of creased blue paper.

Cye idles along the border, left to wonder. There was blood again this morning in the toilet bowl.

He shreds the note and scatters the pieces on the dirt. Thin sheets of clouds, outlined in pink, shade Nunez from the sun as he walks. The farther he goes, through a meadow of stones, the more he shrinks.

Cye says, "*De nada.*"

He jams the Suburban into drive and turns around. Cye rolls slowly over patches of cholla and scrub. There are few signs of anything in the desert. This comforts him for now. Cye knows the route. He's not certain of much. But he knows the direction home.

Little Sins

Jessie and her big plans. Jessie and her big brain, her big job. As always, Jessie's suggestion wins out: Dennis is a Black Pearl. At the drugstore, he argues for Rich Maple, maybe Tawny Bronze. But Jessie insists on the black. The others, she explains, are too close to his natural tones. And what he needs, she goes on, is dramatic change.

At home, his wife applies the last gobs of dye, parting his hair, yanking it. Dennis sits on the toilet while ammonia clouds begin to assault his throat. Finally, when Jessie snaps a shower cap over his head, he panics. Dennis envisions Medusa. Wispy snakelike fumes slithering into his nose, mouth, and eyes, crawling toward the center of his skull. In their poisonous wash of his brainpan, they puncture cells, rip apart wiring. Over time, he's turned mad.

Dennis says, "I feel sick."

"Stop complaining," Jessie says. She unfurls her plastic gloves, pops them into the trash.

"Christ," Dennis says. "This kills. My whole head itches."

"Don't touch for another thirty minutes," Jessie says.

He reaches for his wife's bony hip. He lays a hand there. She is a beautiful woman—blue eyes set in a round face, framed by strawberry blonde hair. For beautiful women, the world changes for them. As if quietly acknowledging this, Jessie slaps his hand away, flicks off the light, and leaves him in the dark.

Dennis wonders when his wife will return. He wonders when she'll put the light back on. He wonders when she'll ever say, "Sorry."

After some time, it becomes clear. Jessie isn't coming back.

A mistress would balance things out, Dennis thinks. From the hall, a glint of light filters in, and Dennis opens a topic he's given sizable consideration. That young receptionist at the nursing home smiles when he walks by. She's cute. Of course, he's the Manager of Operations. She's paid to smile at him.

What feels like fleabites begin needling his scalp. Dennis drops onto the tiles. Already he hates his wife's idea. He riffles through the trash and scans the box of dye. It offers no relief. When he flips the box over, he's stunned. He sees her now clearly, and for the first time: the model on the box.

She's pale, rib-cage thin, with hair soon to be his. Her caught-in-surprise look devours him. Her naked, shiny shoulder beckons. Through teeth as white and straight as piano keys, she says, "Hello."

Dennis has learned to draw pleasure from these small, stolen moments—second-long daydreams that break loose from his world and find another orbit. They're counterbalances against the pieces of Jessie he already knows float free.

In the darkness of the bathroom, another piece loosens, and a name pops into his head. Staring into the young model's hazel eyes, he anoints her with a purpose.

Alexis—that's a good name, an exciting name. And all at once, he tries not to choke.

In the kitchen, Jessie is making lasagna, layering fat noodles into a casserole dish. Condensation has wet the window. Tears skate down the glass.

Dennis sets the table in the nook. In his back pocket, torn from the box, rests the glossy picture of Alexis. The model bolsters him with a thin beam of confidence, which elongates into an incredible need for argument. Lately, he's been carrying around this urge, looking for openings.

"The lasagna," Dennis says. "I hope it's my mom's recipe."

Jessie turns, spatula in hand. "Why do you do that?"

Dennis says, "What?"

"As stupid as it is," Jessie says, "you know how it makes me feel."

Dennis's face melts into mock innocence. "I'm just talking. I like hers. That's all."

"Oh, the man in the shower cap is just talking," Jessie says. "Bullshit. You know how irritating that is."

Now Dennis is provoked. It's the barb in his wife's voice. "So you think I'm irritating?"

"We're talking about me, not you," she says.

So it goes, a fight.

Dennis slams the back door in a mild rage.

The fight does not work out how he hopes. Over the past few months, he's advanced from clumsy to skilled in the mechanics of fighting. He knows how to introduce a trivial annoyance in order to open discussion about the larger—and what he considers cavernous—*problem*. Unfortunately, Jessie knows how to bob and weave.

Dennis falls into a plastic beach chair, striking a match, anticipating his second cigarette of the day. His three-a-day habit has become an excuse to disconnect from the house, detaching from everything inside it.

His suspicions began at her holiday office party. At the bar, a simple graze of pinkies. Later, shared glances from across the room, which struck Dennis as odd.

He remembers everything now in vivid Technicolor, including his introduction to Stephen. It's a scene that plays often, in slow-mo loops, in the theater behind his eyes: his hand lifts, a clammy fish, deadened by alcohol, coldly effete, and it meets awkwardly with a strong athletic claw, which belonged to a man named Stephen.

Dennis daydreams about ripping out his hair, maybe starting over, bald. The shower cap makes him claustrophobic. And he must look pitiful. For a moment he imagines the cigarette drawing close, igniting the cloud of ammonia, followed by a swift burst of flame. His face, and head, left unrecognizable.

The beach chair burps as he shifts. He thinks about this young woman in his pocket, Alexis. He takes out her picture. Their affair would be passionate but short-lived. A dark room, two bodies joining violently, clutching, clutching. They'd drink cheap whiskey from the bottle, smoke French cigarettes in bed. They'd build memories from each stroke and grunt.

Dennis pokes around in the shed. Mildewed boxes cover his old workbench. He meant to build an oak desk once. He only finished a drawer. He also had in mind a shelf for the bedroom. That was before Jessie went out and bought one. His tools look like ancient bones, hanging scientifically from hooks.

Above all, a month after the holiday party, while searching for a dry-cleaning ticket in Jessie's car, he found a ribbed condom in her change compartment, purple colored, warmed from the day's heat, a disgusting, gelatinous little balloon tied at the end to contain, for what reason he still doesn't understand, one hundred million dead sperm that did not belong to him.

Dennis fumbles with his cigarettes. The pack falls, landing with a thud on the shed's concrete. A dull pain blooms in his throat. His lungs are hollow as drums. And look at his tools: everything so fossilized and preserved. He feels himself falling too, his blood to ash, his bones to powder, a cell-by-cell reduction that even warps his fingerprints. Fighting a desire to cry, he tears into his pockets. Lint and a few quarters spill to the ground.

Next to Alexis's picture, at his feet, shines a large bright nail. The nail is solid, clean, perfect.

He stops next to Jessie's black two-door in the driveway. The reflection in the window introduces Dennis to a new Dennis. Apparently, he is a man who now dyes his hair. He's a man who has forgotten he is a man. Or maybe, he is a changing man. He recalls that Stephen also has black, very black, hair.

Jessie's sudden appointments, he thinks. Her late work nights. Most of all, he despises how, as though cleansing herself of sin, Jessie washes her hands when she returns home.

Dennis bends beside his wife's car, and he slides the nail under her rear tire, angling it upward to ensure that it bites.

Five corridors meet at a central nursing desk. Dennis walks up and down each for his midafternoon inspection of the facility. He pauses to help lift Doris from her hunched position. He picks up Rudolph's bowl of pulverized carrots. A lemony antiseptic scent helps conceal a bland, farty aroma that adheres to the walls.

His colleagues at the home have commented on the change. Mostly praise. His hair color works well with his brown eyes. And oh, said the cute young receptionist, how "dark," how "sophisticated."

In the activity room, a volunteer plays "As Time Goes By" on the piano to a room filled with wheelchaired patients. All stare wondrously into space. Ms. Calavert, still somewhat in control of her faculties, is left in charge of the triangle. Every so often, and entirely off-key, she strikes it with a *ting, ting, ting.*

The intercom pages Dennis. A phone call.

"I'm having a shit day," Jessie says.

"Oh?" Dennis says.

"So I'm running out the door to a deposition and my car has a flat. And the spare still hasn't been fixed from last summer."

Dennis listens to his wife's dilemma, growing joyful. She needs him. "I'll take care of it," he says, his voice kick-starting. "Your car's in the parking lot?"

"You'll do that?" Jessie says. "Honey, that would be *tremendous*."

Dennis has always disliked the way Jessie overuses the word *tremendous*. She just loves to throw it around.

"Well, in that case, I'll have someone drive me to the deposition," Jessie says. "We can figure out the rest in the morning. Really, honey, this is *tremendous* of you."

Most of the staff has gone home when Ethel's silhouette shuffles past his door. A walker supports the old woman's willowlike, ninety-five-pound frame. Since she arrived at the home, Ethel's dementia has evolved from progressive to totally blotto. The old woman catches sight of him. She shows off a gapped smile. Dennis is behind his desk.

"Hi, Ethel," Dennis says.

"I'm looking for that boy called my father," Ethel says.

Day after day, comments like this keep Dennis showing up to work.

Dennis says, "You're gone, aren't you?"

"Let me tell you," Ethel says. "This morning I wondered if I should eat my hands or go back to sleep and forget about it."

Dennis says, "I wish there were more Ethels, Ethel."

"Well," Ethel says. But then she's off again. She walks at a snail's pace toward the end of the hall, toward a door plastered with a bright red sign that says DO NOT EXIT, ALARM WILL SOUND.

Ethel has tried this before, and Dennis stands to watch. She pushes the door. Next, she runs a finger along the metal handle, apparently confused. For the first time, she places both hands on the handle, rattling it. Then all at once, a brilliant slice of light shoots inward. The alarm does not sound.

It's a grand moment in Ethel's life. She opens the door wide enough and slithers out. Dennis decides he'll allow her five minutes in the parking lot. Then he'll phone the nursing desk.

Dennis keys a drawer. He pulls out an unopened box of hair dye. He positions Alexis atop a pile of insurance forms. Dennis smiles. Alexis smiles back.

He begins with a simple scene.

An airplane flight. Out beyond the miniscule window, it's a sky full of icebergs. Alexis falls asleep with her head against his shoulder. Her hand is a little ball in his lap. She awakens as they touch down in Montreal. Hands interlaced, they explore the muddy banks of the St. Lawrence River. Dusk approaches and they hop into a carriage. They toss crumbs at fat pigeons.

"I never imagined a sky so purple," Alexis says.

And Dennis says, "Heaven's not far from here."

What a tired cliché! Anxious shock waves stab at him. How unoriginal. God, he used to be so creative. In college, he sculpted rhinoceros penises out of clay. He grew excitable at the mere mention of Hegel. And once, he ate an eighth of hallucinogenic mushrooms, climbed to the top of the campus water tower, and almost fell to his death. Christ, this is what's left?

Dennis shuts his eyes. He tries again. Behind his eyelids, Alexis hooks her leg around him in bed. She says, "Darling?" Her accent is vaguely continental. "Darling," she says, "one more time?"

The tire shop fixes Jessie's flat in an hour. During the drive home, strange palpitations flitter through Dennis as he thinks about the nail's secret little journey, which has ended here, in his shirt pocket.

Jessie is watching a TV program about cats that have undergone amputation. She's sitting on the living room floor, practicing yoga, legs crossed.

"Poor kitties," she says to Dennis. "They're like war kitties. Look, that one's a Sarajevo Ragdoll."

Dennis settles in behind her. He kisses her head lightly. He's met with a mouthful of hair spray.

"Let's add to the family," Jessie says. "We should get a cat."

Dennis produces the nail. He twists the thing between index finger and thumb. He shows it to Jessie as though it's a prize.

"I probably drove through construction," Jessie says.

"Look how long," Dennis says. "I didn't notice how long. Not until now."

He fondles her hair. She seems not to notice. After a while, he lays his hand on her ribs. It's been six weeks since they last had sex. He's been counting.

Finger by finger, Jessie peels his hand away.

She says, "I'm just not . . . there." And then she does what she's so perfect at doing. She turns. She studies him. Hope dissolves in the bowls of her two pitying eyes.

Then, unexpectedly, she grabs his hand and places it back on her ribs. He can almost make out the faint beat of her heart.

While Jessie's in the bathroom, Dennis arranges everything as if he's prepping for surgery. He digs out the vibrator from a drawer. He searches for lube. He finds a towel. Such prep work excited him their first year, perhaps even into their second. Now it's a project. But even though it's a project, he understands the significance of each attempt. It's hard to remember the exact moment he began rooting for her orgasms over his own, but he's certain that his silent cheers intensified after that day he sat alone in Jessie's car, defeat hanging over him like a storm cloud, and placed the used condom back in its hiding place.

Jessie traipses in, wearing a purple bathrobe. She says, "I think I have a bladder infection."

Dennis's desire evaporates. He thinks about the thrill attached to the nail. He stares at the vibrator for a signal. He tries to exploit dirty little thoughts about Alexis. She fails him too.

When Jessie collapses onto the bed, the vibrator jumps. It self-starts. They both look at the thing.

"A good sign?" Jessie says.

Dennis says, "It's something."

After his weak, goopy orgasm, Jessie spreads her arms across his chest. It's been a while since they've nested. His wife is warm and soft. She plays with the hair around his nipples and then, quite suddenly, unbelievably, she descends into a monologue about her "coworker." *Stephen*. How at the office they have such "interesting" conversation. How after his last year of law school, he'll "hopefully" be offered a job. How he ditched school for a semester to backpack abroad. And, oh, by the way, why hasn't Dennis ever tried to climb Mount McKinley, as Stephen has?

Dennis listens through clenched teeth. He stifles a bomb in his stomach, but it quickly detonates with the force of the Big Bang, comes together again through gravitational pull, then re-detonates inside his chest. The holiday office party introduction flashes across time and space and brings the past sweeping to the present: face-to-face with Stephen, the paralegal, at the time an interchangeable office worker in a sea of other office workers, twenty-four years old, green eyes under a shock of black hair, a sideways smirk, the clawed grip, the insect, the wife fucker.

Jessie gets out of bed to pee. When he hears the bathroom door shut, he pillages the kitchen drawers. The nail-in-the-tire trick has left a lingering spark. It's palpable, like kissing live wire.

And has Stephen climbed Mount fucking Everest, too?

Carrying a pair of scissors, he opens the closet. He chooses carefully. Jessie's favorite suits, her blouses, those she likes most. Thread by thread, he snips at the buttons. He clips and clips until the buttons barely hang on. He has to hold himself back. He doesn't want to make it too obvious.

When Jessie returns, Dennis is dressed in his old tracksuit. He's lacing up his tennies.

She eyes him with suspicion. Then she glances at the digital clock. Jessie says, "Are you suddenly taking up jogging?"

"Just going to the shed," Dennis says.

"But it's eleven thirty at night."

"I've been thinking," Dennis says.

"About what?"

Dennis says, "How you build something."

He doesn't finish until two in the morning. He removes the boxes from his workbench. He stacks luggage, brooms, and skis near the back. He cleans his gear with a wet rag, and his hands turn filthy from the work. Finally, he unfolds the cardboard picture of Alexis, the tear-out from the night they met, and he tacks her eye-level on the wall.

———

Jessie hasn't mentioned anything about her blouses, the snipped buttons. Last week, Dennis even handed her one that he'd primed. Still nothing. If she has noticed, she hasn't said a word.

At work, Dennis spaces out to floating boxes on his monitor. He's interrupted by the middle-aged cleaning woman. She's breathless with the news.

"Incorrigibles," the woman says. Shock bathes her face in red. "Someone graffitied the men's room."

Dennis follows her down the hall. She looks to him for signs of disapproval, and he acquiesces with a few slow turns of his head. Yes, it certainly is graffiti, and would you look at that. Clearly, the woman is bothered by how large and red the word MOTHA-FUCKA is, how the red ink contrasts against the white of the tile. And that drawing? A gangly cock overlying two fuzzy, distended peaches? It's just too much for her. Her face suggests a major disturbance in her orderly little world.

"Must be someone's grandkid," Dennis says as they walk back to his office.

"Someone's grandkid?" she says. "This is not the mall." Her wrinkles look as though they might suddenly deepen, fissuring her scowl down the middle.

Dennis says, "I wish I'd thought of it first."

"What?" the woman says. She lays her hand on her chest.

Later, Dennis phones Jessie for a routine check-in. She's in the middle of preparing a motion, she says. Accidentally—on purpose?—she also mentions *his* name, Stephen. Dennis visualizes a grotesque phantom hovering around her office, propelled through the air by a never-ending gush of vomit.

Dennis forces the dull end of a pencil into his palm. He says, oh sure, me too, *busy.*

Before hanging up, Jessie says, by the way, "It's push time. I'll be a little later tonight."

And the line goes dead.

In the back of his mind, Dennis prepares his own motion. An anonymous death threat to Stephen, the paralegal, care of Jenkins, Paul, and Kline. The idea is tasteless, he knows. But it's his, and he holds on to it. It's what he has left. Already he imagines letters clipped from nursing-home trade magazines. Donning latex gloves, tweezers in hand, he sees himself slipping the short, sweet, terrifying note into an envelope and sealing it with a long, glutinous booger.

A Thursday evening, Jessie comes home and the house is spotless. Boxes of Chinese food are aligned like soldiers on the kitchen table. Her clothes are folded neatly on the bed. Her bras and panties are drying on the rack.

Jessie wraps her purse straps around the nub of a chair.

Sipping wine, Dennis says, "Took the day off." He says, "Taking tomorrow off too."

Jessie is tired. Small bags of blue lie under each eye. "You're never going to believe what's happening at work," she says.

"Let's not talk work," Dennis says. He fills a wine glass, slides it across the table. "I ordered the mu shu and hot-and-sour soup," he says.

"So you know Stephen, right?" Jessie says. "My colleague?" Her eyes go wide. "He received this weird threat thing in the mail. We called the police and evacuated the building. People are panicked."

So. Now Stephen's a *colleague*?

Dennis is mildly interested. But his day has been a clean surrender to order. He's vacuumed. He's mopped. He's learned many things about himself, and he doesn't have the energy for this.

"I also ordered the soup dumplings we like," he says.

"You're not listening," Jessie says.

"I listen. Look, I poured wine."

"You don't listen well."

"Well enough," he says. "Look, it's Pinot."

"And why didn't you tell me you took the day off?"

"Well," Dennis says, considering. "When you found out about this whatever, this threat, why didn't you call? You say people are panicked."

Jessie doesn't have a response. And she knows it. It's a delicious moment for Dennis, particularly because he never wins arguments with her. She was born a litigator. He wears these rare moments like a badge. It comes out like a smirk.

Nevertheless, the room goes quiet.

They eat in silence. They pick at noodles with cheap wooden chopsticks. Now his smart-ass point begins to bother him. Why didn't Jessie call? Was she too busy consoling Stephen? Allowing Stephen to cry on her shoulder?

Fuck, Dennis wants to say. *Shit*, he wants to scream. He wants to end the charade, unzip his chest, show off the scars, and then ask his wife *why, please, what for,* and *how many times* and *where?*

Instead, he sips his wine. Jessie refills her glass.

Finally, Dennis says, "Jess. Let's not. We always fight."

"The first to speak," Jessie says.

"I rented a movie," Dennis says. He kicks her shin lightly under the table. "Care to guess what genre?"

"You didn't," she says.

He says, "I did."

"I'm not in the mood," she says.

Not for the past eight months, at least.

"Okay," Dennis says. "A good dinner, though?"

"A good dinner, yes," Jessie says.

Dennis takes refuge on the couch. He dims the lights and waits for the flashes on the screen. After sloppily edited previews, the first scene arrives. Dennis hears Jessie putting away her clothes in the bedroom, shutting drawers loudly. He turns the volume up. Halfway into the second scene, Jessie walks into the living room, and her hand falls from her hip.

"You rented a gay video?" she asks.

An answer is unnecessary, as they both watch one man lick another man's shaved scrotum.

"The box said it got two dicks up," Dennis says.

Jessie studies the TV, unable to formulate a response.

"Come," Dennis says. He pats the couch. "Sit."

His wife stretches out on the floor instead. Eventually, her head rolls back against his thigh. Dennis pets her hair.

As the game once went, they begin with the deconstruction of scenes, commentary on the rise and fall of asses, noting the strange angles, how that must hurt, how that looks fun, all of this before allowing the visuals to trigger their own animal urges. They try again.

Jessie unleashes Dennis's belt, gripping the leather tongue as if choking it. Dennis finds an opening at the back of her skirt. He reaches.

"Look," Dennis says, surprised. He lifts a small black button from the floor. "From your blouse, I think."

Jessie parts her blouse, revealing a gap. "I pay this much and the buttons fall off?"

"I'll get it fixed," Dennis says quickly. He wonders if it came out too quickly.

"And did you dye your hair again?" Jessie says.

"It was a day with nothing to do," he says, running his fingers along her thigh. But unlike a moment before, he's met with heatless shivers.

"It's just . . ." Jessie says. She looks to him as if he contains the answer. As if he contains one simple answer. His wife lifts his hand, pats the back of it, and stands.

"I'm sorry," Jessie says. And she walks out of the room.

The shed is brighter than it's ever been. Cleaner, too; it's a regular workshop. And he needed new lights. The project requires it.

Midnight, Dennis unclasps a thick leather notebook he once meant to use as a journal. It's filled with sketches and diagrams, step-by-step instructions he downloaded from a carpenter's Web site. How to build a six-drawer, double-pedestal, oak desk.

Earlier, he'd purchased the remaining supplies. Ball-bearing slides, three clamping fixtures, oak lumber, and plywood spacers. At the hardware store, he also rented a router table, to be delivered in the morning.

Dennis follows the instructions with childlike determination. He begins with what he didn't finish the previous night and trims the edge of a board. A high, sharp whine from the saw awakens the neighbor's dog. The dog starts barking, in turn sending another neighbor's dog into a frenzy, then another a half block away, until, at last, Dennis finds himself grinning, the conductor of a swelling cacophony.

One weekend morning, Dennis drives the freeway, past the Cineplex, past the city's small airport, toward the brown desert mountains, where he tries to get lost.

Fifty miles from town, he exits. He takes a right, a left. He follows highway lines that lead into the empty desert hills. He slows when he sees wild mustangs feeding on the side of a hill. They are magnificent creatures, and he's struck by a welcome thought. He imagines painting words on the sides of their strong, daunting bodies. They'd make poetry as they raced through the hills.

He pulls off when he spots dunes. The fresh sting of dry desert air awakens him. He climbs until he finds a nice spot. He sets down his blanket, his picnic basket, and sticks the now-laminated picture of Alexis into the sand. For months she's been his companion. There are small scratches across her face.

His fantasy has shifted in scale. Thoughts of Alexis's untried body bring a buzz to his ears. Rather than a hasty affair, it's blossomed into romance. Quick afternoon fucks segueing into long, talkative nights. Their sex is clean, filling. He knows where to press and she knows when to clench. In bed, she reads aloud, passages about ancient cults of the phallus. For fun, he eats skinned grapes from her sunken belly. He slinks a hand underneath her worn college T-shirt, and he's met with sighs. He's familiar with her scent, her rhythms, even the taste of her tears.

Dennis sits with her for a while. He talks to her. He thinks about potentialities: life's paths, his, Jessie's, Alexis and her life, the true her, not just the one he knows.

After a bottle of Pinot, Dennis spreads across the blanket, growing hypnotized by white threads floating through the bright sky. He clenches the picture of Alexis. He rolls to his side. The way he would listen to her. His fingers walk down his groin, triggering a response. And the way Alexis would listen to him. He grips firmly.

Dennis is paged. A nurse hands him a telephone.

"Oh my god, I'm at home, the washing machine finally exploded," Jessie says.

"Okay, calm down," Dennis says.

"The laundry room is flooding," Jessie says. "Water is pouring into the rest of the house. What about our hardwood floors?"

"Calm down," Dennis says.

Jessie says, "I am calm. Will they warp?"

"I'm calling someone now," Dennis says.

"Oh my god, I'm standing in a lake."

"My fingers are on the buttons. I'm dialing them now."

"I have to go back to work," Jessie says. "Can you come home? Fix this?"

He'll be home within the hour, he tells her. He shovels paper-work into an expandable folder. He's furious that Jessie has been home. And in the middle of the day. And for how long? With whom? And washing stains out of what? On good days, her office is a thirty-minute drive one-way.

The laundry room is indeed a lake. Rivulets have also pooled in the kitchen and a portion of the bookcase in the living room is damp. Same with the couch. Dennis yanks the washing machine away from the wall. He discovers a broken pipe. Not his work, unfortunately.

He sheds his tie, finds some old towels, and begins the clean-up. Mementos of his life with Jessie begin to engulf him on all sides. He finds a pair of missing fingernail clippers behind the kitchen door, then a ticket stub from an outdoor performance of *Twelfth Night*. A single pearl earring. As he waddles toward the laundry room, knees aching, he thinks of these objects as lost pieces of a foundation, misplaced artifacts from another world.

There's a second set of wet footprints on the linoleum. Leading here, there, here again. They're larger than Jessie's feet. Dennis checks the pattern on his soles. His. At least they look the same.

The plumber finally arrives. He's a rectangular man. His smile is filled with tobacco-stained teeth.

"This was taped to the door," the plumber says, and he hands Dennis a torn sheet of paper.

You're tremendous, it says.

Dennis finishes the desk's frame earlier than expected. All told, its simplicity surprises him. He's proud of it. He's equally proud of his work space. Everything is arranged neatly. It is a place of use. The stale air from before has traded with the deep musk of wood, the great smell of effort.

He wipes handfuls of sawdust from the workbench. Golden chips sprinkle the floor. Dennis lights a cigarette and takes in the shed. He's amazed by how tangled life can get, how utterly crippled you become when you've worked hard to put something together only to watch as the exterior chips, the center falls out, and you are left holding the pieces.

Taped to the wall, Alexis smirks at him—her standard grin. Her forehead is bent. She's been folded and refolded too many times. There are thick creases along her face, and it appears as though she's aged.

Still, she has a way of looking at him. She smiles a thousand-watt, uncomplicated smile. He has one million questions, he tells Alexis. And he wants one million answers. Pressure builds in his chest; a wound opens there, large enough to last a lifetime.

He tosses the cigarette on the ground. A small bit of comfort comes from watching the thing smolder. It's the giving up of something after it's already been had.

Jessie is reading a thick novel on the couch. Her finger pegs down a page, and her reading glasses have slipped halfway down her nose.

Dennis stands beside the bookcase, dimly lit. He rubs a tiny sliver embedded in his thumb.

Jessie says, "Playing with your tools again?"

She tips her head, looking at him with her large, watery eyes. He's overcome with a desire to carry her to the bedroom. He wants to remove her clothes piece by piece, her socks, her pants, her bra, everything. To feel again the rush as her thighs fall open.

Jessie sighs. It's listless in a way he remembers so well.

"So," Jessie says, blinking twice. "You look like you have something to say."

Mormons in Heat

He that knoweth not good from evil is blameless.
—Alma 29:5, the Book of Mormon

Sunlight flashes off chrome fenders, hitting Eli's eyes, blinding him. Eight motorcycles enlarge in the rearview mirror. Hot this morning, and warming up.

"More highway company," Eli says to Sutton, or to the steering wheel—whichever. This latest cache of sightseeing brochures is simply hypnotizing his partner. Sutton holds one by the edges, handling it like a delicate specimen. Splashed across another glossy pamphlet are different types of cacti.

"Forget about those, Sutton. Pay attention," Eli says. "You might learn something."

As the bikes approach, down goes Eli's window. He wants to

side-glance that fine Harley craftsmanship. He wants to inhale, for a moment, the freedom.

"Chicks on motorcycles," Eli says, clenching the steering wheel. He can almost smell the armpits.

Leading the charge is a woman wearing square gunner's goggles. Eli clocks her at fifty, maybe fifty-five years old. Her cheeks are as red as her flapping bandana, cinched tightly around her skull, and she commands with her chin, which she holds high, with attitude. She veers into the oncoming lane, and Eli marvels at her glistening biceps.

"Elder Sutton," Eli says. "I am experiencing a vision."

Sutton doesn't say anything, not that the kid would. Eli sets his jaw. Why can't he appreciate this impromptu, middle-of-nowhere, wet T-shirt contest? The woman's custom-made turquoise low-rider has high, wide handlebars, and along with a rib-tight T-shirt, she and her companions wear sleeveless leather vests with cartoonish beavers on the back. Over the beaver's crazed, bloodshot eyes and squared buckteeth is the group's name, stitched in white: The Beaver Rockets.

When the last rider thunders past, she opens her throttle and her muffler explodes. Eli's eardrums palpitate. The women soon disappear into the shimmering highway, and again the desert is quiet, cleansed.

"Now that's the work of God," Eli says.

A bead of sweat disappears into Sutton's thin, wordless lips. If the kid has anything to say about what went down the previous night, in Eureka, he's saving it for the Celestial Kingdom.

"She was eighteen," Eli says, stating his case. "So just stop with your dumb look." And there is, always, a look. Sutton has a sharp, lordly nose that goes up whenever he's disappointed.

Eli, recalling what happened, grows tense and aroused. Desert daughters love opening their legs. He's learned that. He was two nights in Eureka when he met Emily, Emily Something-or-Other. The girl was a threat to any man with functioning testes: strawberry-flavored, bee-stung lips and a stomach as firm as watermelon rind. Last night, he fast-talked the girl out of a pair of rose-print panties. Then, this morning, shocked to realize his bareback, condomless mistake, he unleashed an incoherent but firm speech, insisting that she ingest six blue, oval, morning-after pills. Quite lucky, he lied to the pretty young stranger, he just so happened to work in pharmaceuticals.

"Guilty as charged," Eli says. "She was my Achilles. I admit it. Can we drop it?"

The missionaries flew out of Eureka, coursing along the furnace of Pancake Range. After a wrong turn back on 375, the so-called Extraterrestrial Highway, Eli flipped a U and decided on 95 instead. He's aiming for distance, after all. Highway 95 is as flat and coppery as a penny.

Near Goldfield Summit, Eli stops to refuel at a highway gas shack. Prolonged drives make his muscles feel itchy and needled. He scours the trunk for his racquetball, something to squeeze. With all these Books of Mormon they ferry around, there's hardly space for luggage. A canister of motor oil has leaked all over one box. And, thanks to Sutton, the trunk is also filthy with brochures. Hundreds of them! Sutton collects and actually reads the stupid things, front to back. Eli's come across one from every county, an advertisement for Virginia City's Suicide Table, maps of isolated ghost towns. They've never been to Pyramid Lake or the Area 51 Mountaintop Lookout, and, Eli decides, they never will.

"Seen my racquetball?" Eli says, tapping Sutton's window. He mimes like he's rolling down an imaginary window.

Sutton throws a cold glance at him before returning to his brochure.

"Jesus. Let's not rush to the podium," Eli says.

Just look at the kid. Buttoned-up in a starched white shirt and a navy blue blazer. Scarecrow thin, size twenty-eight waist, Sutton could pass for thirteen. And his military-style haircut and glassine features certainly don't add any years. Oh, Sutton is Salt Lake City's foot soldier, all right. On hundred-plus days, during long hauls, he dresses in the required uniform. Even his goddamn name badge is always pinned on, per Church regulations.

Whatever sadist at HQ paired him with Sutton should be fired. After spending an entire year alone, the Church finally delivered

Eli a partner. His partner turned out to be a dud. Eli wondered if he could ship him back. He was told that the kid was "shy." But Sutton isn't "shy." He's pathologically withdrawn. Sutton has only spoken a few dozen paragraphs, at most, but the sentences in those paragraphs aren't strung together. Each remark arrives startlingly, unattached to further conversation, each awkward syllable as unlikely as a snowflake landing in Death Valley.

When Sutton isn't looking, Eli scoops up an armful of pamphlets. He deposits them in a nearby trash can.

Eli settles behind the wheel, next to his monkish partner. Eli once read a magazine article about a man with severe epilepsy. Surgeons had to remove half of the guy's brain. When the patient awoke, he learned that the empty side of his cranium was filled with Ping-Pong balls. Three strands of light blond hair are caked to Sutton's forehead. Eli starts the car, wondering what's in there.

Eli has maintained a steady level of paranoia throughout his tour, sure that the higher-ups are watching him, keeping tabs. Hardwired in his DNA is the fuck-up gene. He understands this. It's always been his way. Surveillance could have started the moment he slaughtered his compulsory vows. Odd the way his sponsor, guy by the name of Jeremiah, never took him seriously after that.

Eli thinks about it from time to time. Perhaps he was a little too eager to enlist in the Church of Jesus Christ of Latter-Day Saints. And maybe he was too pushy by insisting on a mission. After all, LDS didn't find him. He flipped open the Yellow Pages and he dialed them. It was either LDS or the Jehovahs, Eli didn't care, but a nearby LDS Ward called back first. After his endowment ceremony, Church officials must have been stumped. What to do with a thirty-year-old, jobless divorcé who's been living in his brother's basement? Save his soul, yes. But send him where?

Eli excels at putting distance between himself and his problems. Take what happened with Margo, his ex-wife, for example. One affair at his real estate office melted into the next. Margo found out and yeah yeah: divorce. That made *número dos*. Shit, he needed to get his act together. Not long after she walked out (actually, she made him leave), he began paying more attention to the Church's bland TV commercials. LDS appeared to be a wholesome enough choice.

And his decision worked—for a while. The Church kept him on track his first year out in the desert. Eli actually began believing in this stuff. The Books were all around him, so he began to read. Salvation through purity through family seemed okay by him. He was cruising through this missionary thing. He was giving away Books faster than headquarters could ship them FedEx.

Of course, there were a lot of smoky bars amid the brush weed. Also lots of press-on fingernails in those honky-tonks. After pounding pavement morning till night, there was little for Eli to do in those backward towns in the middle of Nevada. The red-haired, bowlegged woman worked for the Bureau of Land Management. Her job, she explained, was exterminating a particular species of invasive thistle. Not that it mattered. What mattered was the morning he awoke next to her, her salty toe lodged in his mouth.

His budding faith incrementally flaked away, bleached by the sun, stripped off by harsh desert wind. Nothing was left for Eli back in Texas, in Houston, his hometown. Rather than abandoning his mission, he stayed the course. He remained in the desert. Besides, everything was all-expenses-paid. Looked at properly, he was enjoying an extended, two-year vacation.

All he had to do was dispense the Books. The Church was always sending him more, and still more, goddamn Books. He scattered them in places named Jackpot, Battle Mountain, and Manhattan, Nevada.

Highway speed signs read seventy, so Eli goes eighty-five. He wants half the state between him and this morning. That feat in Eureka has that one-two-three strikes ring to it. He thinks the stunt is grounds for excommunication. Eli mashes his heel into the accelerator.

Mud lakes and sand flats skate past the windows. A sea of sagebrush blurs into silver-green fog. Sun fries Eli's knuckles. Augusts are miserably hot. Nevada is long empty roads, etched ridgelines, so much open blue.

Plastic grocery bags trapped by sage introduce the town of Amargosa, a minor highway pit stop cuddled by low hills. Eli slows down when he realizes the town is crawling with bikers.

Eight lady joyriders on a lonely desert highway are a welcome sight. But sixty-plus middle-aged women dangling from ape-hanger handlebars, their modified Hogs parked along the town's half-mile drag, make for an unexpected, discombobulating weirdscape. Amargosa is firing on all cylinders. It's as though he and Sutton have penetrated some sort of menopausal biker pod. Drug-thin gals in tight-tight Tees idle next to large-boned women squeezed into jeans. Frontward denim pouches hold beery guts. Some of the women look terrifying, notably the gray-haired lady wearing the "Priestess" T-shirt.

Eli pulls to the side of the road, stunned.

"We have to keep driving," Sutton says unexpectedly. The kid blinks like there's sand in his eyes.

"You work," Eli says. "Did I forget to wind you?"

Sutton reaches for the gearshift, but Eli slaps at his knuckles. "Jesus H," Eli says. So many women, he wants to say. He says instead, "You are the worst evangelical I've ever met." He points out the window. "These are potential converts."

A Hi-Top Motel sits across the street. Three big-breasted women are loitering on the upper balcony. They're huddled around a ripped-open twelve-pack of beer. One of them waves, and Sutton blinks spastically.

Each small, desert town is a slow-mo rerun of the previous dusty stop, full of tedious chitchat and hundreds of miles before interesting new faces. It isn't a hard decision to make.

"We're staying the night," Eli says. "Too many hours behind the wheel," he says. "Plus, my heels ache." He cracks his large toe.

In the motel's air-conditioned office, Sutton plucks brochures from a plastic rack. Not surprisingly, he's holding up his nose. The kid scrutinizes one brochure with a frog across its cover. He swipes several others and slips them into his blazer.

Thanks to the flock of bikers, it's the Hi-Top's last room. Every Hi-Top has the same flavor: bolted down TVs and cheap sunset wallpaper. This particular room smells like a difficult case of athlete's foot. Eli thinks it would be nice, just once, to open the door onto an ocean view. Oh to be able to inhale eucalyptus.

Sutton sheds his blazer and retreats to the bathroom, taking his brochures with him. He slams the door.

Most baby-faced nineteen-year-olds are awarded the primo assignments, two years' traveling around Argentina, Switzerland, the tropics. Eli, on the other hand, knew he was eleven years past the expiration date. A different set of rules applied. On the day he was given his Divine Assignment, he was escorted into a back room of his local Ward. He was handed a worn map of Nevada, keys to a used Toyota, and a credit card good at any Hi-Top Motel in the southwestern United States. The Church, he was quietly informed, was a majority shareholder.

The small parking lot is overrun with custom-made motorcycles. Eli stands gaga at the window. His lips are brackish from the long, face-melting drive, and he feels dehydrated, which always gives him a buzz. Mufflers rumble distantly.

The Beaver Rockets. He's never heard of the motorcycle club, or whatever they are. He spots the woman from the highway, Ms. Biceps, Ms. Red Bandana, holding court from the seat of her low-rider. Her bandana has disappeared, revealing licorice-black hair fashioned into a mullet, business in the front and party in the back. Others listen as she puffs on a cigar. The next time she lifts the stogie to her lips, clutching it, Eli's knees weaken. His thoughts drift. He imagines a life similar to hers, beside hers, without rules—gnats in his eyes, unpaid bills, arrest warrants with his name on them.

Eli's only successful conversion happened his first week, a Western Hemisphere record. Only one other missionary ever saved another soul within the first seven days. But that was in 1977, in Phuket, Thailand, a different landmass, with completely different standards. So as far as Eli is concerned, it doesn't count. He wins.

For his record breaker, he brought around a copper-mine fore-man from Cactus Springs named Ted Ringle and his non-English-speaking wife, Tanja. Ted Ringle explained, with a wink, that his new bride was mail-ordered and arrived via Turkish freighter.

Anyway, Eli was out to cut his teeth. He had something to prove. Fresh off a divorce, anointed with a purpose, he was soldier-ready.

For a week he showed up at the Ringles' apartment with Mini Mart donuts. After reading the usual, best-of, all-time-greatest LDS hits from the Book, Eli would bow his head and say, "Let's pray." Good-spirited Ted Ringle would nod while his Slavic wife smiled. Bless her heart: she understood nothing. And whenever Ted Ringle posed one of the big, unanswerable questions, Eli would pinch his chin and say, "That is interesting. That is very interesting." Eli learned the importance of validating without answering.

The newlyweds for Eli were a coup. They were everything the Church wanted, a happy, healthy couple on the verge of procreation. But after his first converts, Eli's luck ran out.

So he fine-tuned his advance. He tailored his routines. Each mark required a fresh approach. Conversion was a delicate con. Assumed godliness, thankfully, commanded a modicum of respect. If he had God on his bench (or when others thought he might have God on his bench), they sometimes listened.

Where to find the people, the hearts and minds, the converts? He attended town hall meetings, county fairs, and small-time rodeos. It took patience to sniff out the most attentive audiences.

Lonely old farts were a great discovery. They couldn't hurry away. On Saturday evenings, state-run nursing homes rolled out the bingo and pinochle, and Eli would show up, his face red and raw from having just shaved, and he'd wander around pretending to be a lost grandson.

Naturally, old folks enjoyed their tall tales, too. Eli began to loathe the countless variations on World War II, childhood in Kansas, how-things-were yarns. He was shown plenty of embroidery and too much needlepoint. Then he began noticing the vultures, vultures of all sizes, during his long treks around the state. Their talons were always curled around power lines, perched as though recharging. The ugly birds fed off the weak. They too took advantage of soon-to-be carcasses.

Eli cooled it on the geriatrics. He returned to rural ranches and neighborhood grids. Dressed as he was, in a navy blue spokesperson getup, a square, white name badge over his heart, he was a spot-on giveaway. The sight of him inspired grimaces. Women were nicer than men, and mothers he could talk to. But whenever one of them balked, he'd let loose with the scare routine.

"War, Ma'am," he'd begin. "This is war. And you and your lovely daughter here are in a foxhole. A hot bullet rips through her eye. That creamy scarlet hole is a horror show. That's right. Her eye hangs down her face like some broken jack-in-the-box coil. Bombs are concussing. Your daughter is moaning. So do you take Him into your heart? *Do you then?* To save your daughter's eternal soul?"

Rumor has it there are special departments in Hell set aside for the Sons of Perdition. If only Eli believed in quote-unquote Hell, if he just believed in quote-unquote the Sons of Perdition, he might be frightened away from his boozy mistakes. He was counting on the Church to clear the brush from his yard. Hellfire scare tactics work on others. Why not him? He knows officials in SLC wouldn't be pleased with his antics. Hell, they'd probably throw a few aneurisms.

Eli shuffles across the grubby motel carpet. He taps the wood of the bathroom door with his uncut fingernails.

"We haven't even touched these new boxes," Eli yells through the door. "What do they expect us to do? Eat them?" He's referring to the latest shipment. "I'm going out. Want me to grab some local leaflets? The usual?"

He hears the sound of a toilet flush. As usual, Sutton doesn't respond. Eli presses his palm to the door. He doesn't like Sutton. He doesn't understand him. Still, he feels somewhat protective of the kid. It's the same disturbing feeling that overcomes him whenever his brother leaves Eli alone with his retarded, helmet-protected nephew.

In the bathroom of the local Bongo Burger, Eli squeezes out

drops of lingering guilt piss, inhaling the medicinal stench off the urinal puck.

He sets a gold-embossed Book on the toilet's lid in the first stall. He puts another in the adjoining stall. He leans one more against the faucet. Customers will have to move them. People love free things, right? Lately, this has been Eli's general strategy. Who cares if some anonymous face then pops a Book or two in the trash? Not his problem. He's got all these goddamn Books. HQ keeps sending him these fucking Books.

There's not a single cloud in the sky, and an eastern breeze drifts in carrying traces of smoldering sage. Sweat that hasn't absorbed into Eli's sacred garments settles in a wet sack around his groin. He's in a constant fight against rashes. He calls the long, funny underwear, which wraps his torso and ends at his knees, his Brigham Sweatbox.

Eli finds two metal newspaper boxes on Amargosa's strip of boarded-up storefronts. The *Daily Wart* sits beside a national newspaper with week-old headlines. He shovels a few Books on top of the national paper and the spring-loaded door slams shut. Yet another lazy tactic—but whatever.

As he's propping the other box open, a motorcycle appears alongside the curb. Its rim is polished to a mirror finish. Ms. Former Red Bandana, Ms. Cigar Toker, Ms. Woman of the Highway, holds a bottle of beer.

"Toss me a paper?" she says to Eli. Two lime-green eyes, hooded by wild, untended eyebrows, overwhelm him. He stares at her like he's stupid.

"A newspaper please," she says again. She points at the local, the *Daily Wart*.

He fumbles, handing one over. Up close, the woman's triceps are stunning. Deep ravines line the backs of her arms. Her crinkly neck is absurdly out of place with the rest of her, or vice versa.

"Tina Pennybocker," she says to Eli in a rasp. "Tina was born in Amargosa."

She folds back the paper, and he's shown a thumbnail photo of a brunette with spectacular bangs. The brunette's hair crests like a breaking wave. It's a face only a mother could love. Unfortunately for Tina Pennybocker, her photo lies in the center of the obituaries.

"Tina's family plot is down the road at the cemetery," the woman tells him. "A damn shame the nearest minister lives in Tonopah. He called Joanna. Said he can't make it. None of us have much to do in the way of what he's about."

She runs her thick fingers through her mullet and takes a swig of her beer. There's a sudden thirst in Eli's throat. His uvula aches. Dusty goggles hang around the woman's furrowed neck, nestled inside loose cleavage, a soft, flabby, freckled wonderland.

His shirttails aren't tucked. Mustard stains decorate his collar, and his dress shoes are laughably tattered. His LDS name badge is long gone too, misplaced somewhere at Massacre Lake during an all-night bonfire with three Paiutes. He looks anything but pious. Still, getting interested, he glances again at the woman's low-cut landscape.

He says, "Actually, you're in luck." He places a Book on her rhinestone-encrusted saddleback. "I might be able to help," he says. "Eli," he tells her.

The woman's smile shows off a brown front tooth, a shade darker where it meets her gums. Eli always likes people better when they're a little broken.

"Your name?" he asks, and he gently takes her beer bottle. Church doctrine dictates absolutely no alcohol.

"Jane," the woman says. Then she adds, as though it's her surname, "from Wyoming."

Church doctrine also states no fornication outside the sacred bonds of marriage.

"The Lord visits us in unexpected ways," Eli says to Jane-from-Wyoming. He swallows a mouthful of piss-warm beer. That mouthful tells Eli he'd very much like another, and soon.

Nights like this, shrouded by amber lamplight, the idea of a next day does not exist. Jane-from-Wyoming chisels him down to basics. With her, he is just muscle, nerve, and nuclei. All night, motorcycles roam the street, their exhaust notes like Gatling guns, upending Eli's whiskey-sugared dreams.

Their brief get-to-know-you joyride into the tan hills beyond Amargosa segued into shots, cigarettes, and nibbles off of her briny Wyoming neckline. Jane-from-Wyoming smells of seaweed, and when he melts into her large, lumpy breasts, he imagines swimming in an oil slick. Plaquelike odor rises from her decaying tooth, and her expert tongue probes like a lizard's.

In the middle of the night, Eli jolts awake. He sits upright. His throbbing erection pushes against the heavy bedspread. He is insanely thirsty; did he eat a sand castle? The room looks wicked, strange, as though he's seeing it for the first time through smudged blue lenses. Odd, too, the last time his rectum throbbed a doctor was checking for a leaky appendix.

Sutton marches out of the bathroom in tighty-whiteys. He wears only one sock. A bright fluorescent bulb illuminates steam billowing from the kid's shoulders. Like always, he's been showering, his favorite pastime when Eli's busy. Sutton pulls a cover from the other bed and yanks it into the bathroom.

Eli pinches up the sheet and studies his bedmate's cream-cheese body. Varicose veins line her thighs. He might as well be looking at a map of the country's interstate highway system. He is horror-struck. He is so turned on.

A night with Jane-from-Wyoming isn't life changing, but he will have to reevaluate things. At one point, he was sort of tossed in the air and thrown against the headboard, which accounts for his aching jaw. It feels like it's been broken and reset. The floor, strewn with condoms, is a spring-break shoreline. Jane-from-Wyoming snores like a trucker.

She rolls over, taking the rest of the sheets with her. Eli freezes. How to turn the troublesome thing off? He needs a switch. She rolls again, and her hand lands on his sternum. As if sensing its animal heat, her fingers wander downward. She steers him like he's a joystick, a game, an object. He is powerless under her weight.

In the morning, Sutton struts out of the bathroom, showered, dressed, and toothpasty. The knot in his tie is a perfect Windsor. The sight of his partner's early morning efforts rouses Eli's nausea.

"We're leaving," Eli says to Sutton. Eli rolls out of bed and begins picking clothes off the floor. There's a window in the bathroom. It's small, but they'll fit through. For some reason, Sutton starts arranging brochures on the other bed, fanning them out, situating them . . . just so. The kid probably read each one—fascinating!

"Are you showing the place?" Eli asks, growing more irritated. He can't find his necklace, a gold crucifix, his Grapapa's.

Jane-from-Wyoming, bless her, tumbled out of the room before dawn. And she never returned. Eli parts the drapes. Beaver Rockets are gathering in the parking lot. He quickly shuts them. Sutton hovers with that nose of his.

"I don't need your jury-foreman attitude," Eli says. "I'm in the middle of a crisis. My grandfather's necklace. It's gone."

"You told her you're giving the sermon," Sutton says.

Eli snorts. How many lies has he used, and with less muscular women? He throws open the end table, and inside is a new bible. Those goddamn Gideons. Eli's smacked with admiration. They are on top of it.

"That's pent-up sperm talk," Eli says to Sutton. "I'm not giving any sermon. In fact, we're leaving. Right now."

"You said," Sutton says. "I heard you through the door."

"Hallelujah, you talk," Eli says. "A miracle."

This new pain feels like studded plates pressing into his temples. Not to mention, Eli's left incisor is chipped. A quart of Blue Label: just about the right amount for him to tell Jane-from-Wyoming he'd give a sermon. Eli detests public speaking. Anxiety logjams the sentences in his throat before they ever reach open air.

Chewing on the side of his thumb, Sutton paces a figure eight. His willowy shoulders slump forward, and he looks exactly like the teenager that he is. The Church dispatches its lambs when they're only nineteen, the crucial years, when a young man's hard-on is at its hormonal and optimal peak. But Eli doesn't think Sutton ever ties off his own rope. They've shared the same room every night for the past one hundred fifty nights, their pillows mere yards apart, and Eli's never seen movement, or heard rustling, underneath Sutton's sheets.

Eli realizes he's laced his shoes wrong. He skipped holes on both feet. Already it's a horrible start.

Sutton says, "We're going to that woman's funeral."

Another divorce, followed by this missionary charade, barrels of bad decisions, and now that Sutton is finally speaking, he's high-minded. The total prick.

"I like you better when you're broken," Eli says. "Please shut up."

A wolfish glint lights up the kid's eyes. His shoulders pull back and his spine straightens. He charges over. Eli raises his arms in self-defense. But rather than a fist, Sutton comes up with a pair of size 16 panties. They're yellow. He squashes them into Eli's nose.

"I know," Eli says. He sits on the bed. "I know, I know. This is worse than the hooker in Mesquite, isn't it?"

A large contingent of beaver insignias has colonized the Hi-Top's parking lot. Eli's stomach drops when he sees this. More arrived during the night. Sutton shoves Eli out the door, where Jane-from-Wyoming is waiting next to her turquoise bike. Frayed denim cutoffs accentuate her strong, cellulite-padded thighs.

"You clean up," she says. Jane-from-Wyoming looks rested, considering.

"Splashed water in my eyes," Eli says.

Jane-from-Wyoming pats her hump seat. "Minister."

Eli hates her. Eli adores her. He feels chapped bodywide.

"I said," she says. Her lip rises like a curtain, parading her ugly tooth.

As he straddles the seat, Sutton thrusts a bible at him. It's from the end table, those overachieving Gideons.

The kid says to him, "Do good."

A meandering motorcade has formed on the street. They drive to the front, assuming the lead. The smell of burnt asphalt yields to whiffs of peppermint coming off Jane-from-Wyoming's shampooed mullet.

A beat-up hearse soon rolls into town. Fingers point down the road, directing it to the lead spot, where Eli's afforded a first-rate view, beyond tinted glass, of a plain brown coffin. He's unable to attach any feelings to the thing. To him it's just a large box, nothing more. But he is startled when the driver suddenly leaps out, both thumbs raised, smiling wildly. Short, Latino, the guy's dressed in orange sweats. His socked feet are shoved into a pair of checkered, slip-on Vans with demolished heels. He wears them more like flip-flops, scraping the pavement as he walks. Obviously, the guy is thrilled to be around so much fringed leather and feathered hairdos. Eli's relieved when he sees Sutton, behind the wheel of the Toyota, at the rear of the motorcade.

"I apologize for taking advantage," Jane-from-Wyoming says over her shoulder. She squeezes his knee. "You're a man of the cloth. I understand. But there are times a woman needs a mercy fuck. Tina was a dear friend."

Eli says, for lack of anything, "Glad I could help."

"The bite marks will disappear," Jane-from-Wyoming adds. Before he can respond, she stabs the air with her fist. Engines rev, the deep reverberations begin. Eli's brain rattles in his skull. His testicles vibrate on the seat. He imagines this is how war sounds, mechanized and unrelenting.

The deafening swarm follows the hearse a quarter mile and turns down a dirt road, ending at Amargosa's cemetery, nothing more than a powdery scrap of land dotted with scorched weeds. Dominating an acre's worth of headstones is a granite obelisk engraved with the dead woman's name: PENNYBOCKER. It overlooks a sad excuse for a river. Eroded banks hold gray pools of stagnant water. Etched thickly at the base of the monument is the father's generic name, Edward William. Eli does the math on him. Dead twelve years. Her mother, Helen Douglas, followed seven years later. Plenty of room for Tina's four easy letters.

Four women with arms as burly as Jane-from-Wyoming's wrestle the casket from the hearse. They throw it onto a hoist perched over a freshly dug grave. The driver claps, slipping out of his shoe.

Eli can't find Sutton anywhere in the crowd. As the women gather, angling for position, shoulder to shoulder, he wonders how many more predicaments, how many more can he stomach? Deliver a sermon? Eli doesn't even know how, or why, Tina Pennybocker of Amargosa died. He figures he'll just say, Bless this, Bless that, Too bad for Tina, rev the Toyota's four cylinders, and haul ass out of town—next stop Elko.

These expectant eyes might as well be dentist drills. His heart beats in his throat, nearly sealing it. And his stomach squirts up a teaspoon's worth of bile onto the back of his tongue. He is 100 percent hangover emotional. Noxious exhaust fumes from the bikes swirl, and the glare off some lady's tachometer makes his eyes water.

Eli struggles, and he says, "The sky is hustling with light."

Hustling with light?

He finds faith difficult, if not impossible. Sure, he'd like to believe. When he signed the forms, when he joined the Church, Eli thought it might get the ball rolling. But it didn't. It hasn't.

He peers out over the mob of women. Pale morning light reddens above the hills. It's a commanding land, that's certain. Heat and infinite, forever sky. The West does have the best views. Nothing is more sacred than the sun, he thinks, spotlight on us all.

"Let us look up," Eli says. And a few naïve women actually do. His throat catches when he says, "Up at the sky." A sun-glare tear drips down his cheek. Jane-from-Wyoming, misinterpreting, lays her hand between his shoulder blades.

"It's not easy," she says, "I know." Eli briefly recalls the sensation of cold keys whipping his bare ass.

There's a tug on Eli's shoulder, and Sutton steps forward, his sleeves rolled up, lips pursed, his nose raised high. The teenager clutches the brochure with the frog on the cover. He stands before the women assuredly, as if, Bible open, he's behind a pulpit.

"Kid," Eli says.

Sutton stares back at him coolly, and then calmly, reading from his trifold brochure, he begins.

"Amargosa is home to one of the rarest forms of life in the world. Here, along a twelve-mile stretch of river, off Highway 95, down the road from Bud's World-Famous Sausages on a Stick, lives the Amargosa toad." The kid pauses, scanning the vellum paper with his thumb. The sun turns his hair entirely white.

"Amargosa toads are chubby and covered with warts," he goes on. "They're often different colors, beige or olive green, and always have a trim stripe decorating the back. Distinct for webbed toes, for tinted humps, and for black spots on its belly, this ugly but humble creature is truly one of nature's more peculiar sights."

Eli's clenched teeth begin aching.

"I didn't know Tina Pennybocker," the kid says, folding the brochure. "I didn't know there was a Tina Pennybocker until recently. But when I look at you, her friends, the grieving, it's clear that Tina Pennybocker was like the Amargosa toad." One woman releases a high gasp. The kid quickly says, in conclusion, "She was rare. Tina was special."

This draws appreciative sighs. Eli spots the Toyota out of the corner of his eye. He maps out a tiptoe escape route. Nearby, a breeze spins up a dust devil. Space opens up behind him, and he takes a step backward.

Tina's casket is lowered into the grave via steel crank, dusted soon after by fistfuls of dirt. Teary women line up and take turns bidding farewell.

Eli shuffles, he bobs, he weaves. While hiding behind a broad-shouldered woman, a safe distance from all the sobbing, he watches Jane-from-Wyoming tug at her shirt and scratch her collarbone. Wrapped around her thick, dinosaur-sized neck is a gold necklace, a crucifix. His. Grapapa's.

Eli says, "Oh, sweet fucking Christ."

A woman turns and shushes him. There's a chrysanthemum tattooed inside the rim of her ear, the only flower at the service.

Eli snaps his fingers, trying to signal Sutton. Instead, Jane-from-Wyoming notices him hiding behind one of her friends. A look of confusion spreads across her face and then rearranges into benevolence. Jane-from-Wyoming half-smiles. That tooth, so imperfect, so him.

THE IOWA SHORT FICTION AWARD AND JOHN SIMMONS SHORT FICTION AWARD WINNERS, 1970–2007

Donald Anderson
Fire Road
Dianne Benedict
Shiny Objects
David Borofka
Hints of His Mortality
Robert Boswell
Dancing in the Movies
Mark Brazaitis
The River of Lost Voices:
Stories from Guatemala
Jack Cady
The Burning and
Other Stories
Pat Carr
The Women in the Mirror
Kathryn Chetkovich
Friendly Fire
Cyrus Colter
The Beach Umbrella
Jennifer S. Davis
Her Kind of Want
Janet Desaulniers
What You've Been Missing
Sharon Dilworth
The Long White
Susan M. Dodd
Old Wives' Tales
Merrill Feitell
Here Beneath Low-
Flying Planes
James Fetler
Impossible Appetites
Starkey Flythe, Jr.
Lent: The Slow Fast
Sohrab Homi Fracis
Ticket to Minto: Stories
of India and America
H. E. Francis
The Itinerary of Beggars

Abby Frucht
Fruit of the Month
Tereze Glück
May You Live in
Interesting Times
Ivy Goodman
Heart Failure
Ann Harleman
Happiness
Elizabeth Harris
The Ant Generator
Ryan Harty
Bring Me Your Saddest
Arizona
Mary Hedin
Fly Away Home
Beth Helms
American Wives
Jim Henry
Thank You for Being
Concerned and Sensitive
Lisa Lenzo
Within the Lighted City
Renée Manfredi
Where Love Leaves Us
Susan Onthank Mates
The Good Doctor
John McNally
Troublemakers
Kevin Moffett
Permanent Visitors
Lee B. Montgomery
Whose World Is This?
Rod Val Moore
Igloo among Palms
Lucia Nevai
Star Game
Thisbe Nissen
Out of the Girls' Room
and into the Night